FINS

A JAKE SULLIVAN NOVEL

THE JAKE SULLIVAN SERIES

Come Monday

Trying to Reason with Hurricane Season

Havana Daydreamin'

A Pirate Looks at Forty

One Particular Harbour

Son of a Son of a Sailor

Jamaica Mistaica

Changes in Latitudes, Changes in Attitudes

He Went to Paris

Tampico Trauma

Fins

ALSO AVAILABLE:

Trilogy

The First Ten Adventures

COMING SOON:

Big Rig

FINS

A JAKE SULLIVAN NOVEL

CHIP BELL

"Can't you feel 'em circlin' honey
Can't you feel 'em swimmin' around?
You got fins to the left, fins to the right,
And you're the only bait in town."

- "Fins"
by Jimmy Buffett

DEDICATION

To Charlotte Rose, our little sweetie.

ACKNOWLEDGEMENT

To Eve, for simply being Eve, and to all the people who have been kind enough to read the first ten volumes of this series ... I hope you enjoy this one and the rest to come.

PROLOGUE

CITY OF TENOCHTITLAN, LAKE TEXCOCO

MARCH 1520

CHAPTER 1

Montezuma II stood on the balcony of the Royal Palace in the capital city of the Aztec Empire. He had come to realize that those he had welcomed as gods, even believing their leader to be the great Quetzalcoatl, were not gods, but devils, concerned only with the precious metals and jewels stored in their treasury.

It was a clear night with a slight breeze, and he saw the flames flickering on the torches that lit the canals as canoes moved slowly through the city. He gazed north and saw the great star that, hopefully, would lead the way for the fleet that was moving across the sea to the mighty river that would take them to their ancient home. If all worked as he hoped, he would take all his people there, and they would begin the empire anew in the land of their beginnings, where the ancient temple rose out of the shallow sea fed by the three rivers.

The devils and their leader, Cortes, as he had learned, had left to go fight a war on the southern coast, and he had seized the opportunity.

He knew the devils were not gone for good and would return. Their lust for the wealth of his treasury was overwhelming.

He had sent a hundred of his bravest men on a trek north by land, leaving a trail that anyone could follow. They had taken only a small amount of the treasury's wealth with them and had been instructed to leave items, as if lost, for the devils to find as they pursued the object of their transgression in his land.

The remaining vast majority of the treasury had been taken by an army of warriors over land to the northern coast, where an armada of much larger canoes were kept at the ready, under guard. These constantly moved back and forth across the open sea, trading and, sometimes, fighting with and conquering tribes in the northern land. These would be filled with the treasure and then moved across the open sea to the great river, which would take the treasure back to the ancient temple, where it would be stored until such time as the Aztec people could return.

The men in each group would, in stages, ultimately, fight to the death, the last man killing himself, so the secrets of their separate paths would remain only with him. If the devils refused to follow the trail north, he would drive them from the land and then take his people home. Tomorrow there would be a sacrifice to the gods where he would ask for success, and then he would await the return of Cortes and his army, and the gods would seal their fate.

But gods have plans of their own, and in four short months, Montezuma would be dead and the Aztec treasure would be lost to time and legend.

GRINDER'S STAND, NATCHEZ TRACE

OCTOBER 1809

CHAPTER 2

Meriwether Lewis, Governor of the Louisiana Territory, knew his time was short. He had been a fool to allow Neelly, an Indian agent whom he had discovered was an informant of Wilkinson and Burr, to join him at Chickasaw Bluffs, when he changed his plans from taking the Mississippi to New Orleans and then sailing to Washington. In addition to a British blockade, he was concerned that men aligned with Wilkinson and Burr would be waiting for him, and he would never get through to see former President Jefferson.

His thinking was clouded by the fever and he had forgotten that his subordinate, a traitor, Frederick Bates, had mentioned Neely in one of the many letters he had confiscated . . . letters that tied them both to General James Wilkinson and Aaron Burr in their treasonous attempt to join with Spain in creating a new country of their own in the Louisiana Territory.

More importantly, he carried other documentation . . . documentation of the greatest discovery of his career . . . a discovery that would forever change his country . . . a discovery he had to make known to Jefferson.

He walked outside the cabin into the cool night air, splashed his face with water from the trough, and tried to clear his mind. The fever would not leave him, just as it had not left Clark when he had returned to their camp at Three Forks, the headwaters of the Missouri. Perhaps it was the ancient gods protecting their secret, but he, Meriwether Lewis, had conquered any curses they may have left behind. Let them slander him about his land speculating, his financial state, his clothing, and his appearance. He and only he had been able to recognize the great plateau for what it was. Only he had discovered the chalice, covered with a layer of silt in the riverbed of the Jefferson, and only he had the imagination to realize what it might mean and to pursue it until the discovery was his.

He again shook his head to clear the cobwebs and returned to the cabin, where, by candlelight he composed a letter to Jefferson.

When he had finished, he put down the quill and read it to himself.

"To His Excellency, President Jefferson,

I, your most humble servant, hope
that you will have the opportunity to read
this, my last letter directed to you.

I fear that by the time it is in your
hands I will be dead, at the hands of those
who would put their own interest above that
of our beloved nation.

If this information makes its way to
you through the efforts of my honest and
loyal servant, John Pearny, you will see
the documentation I have amassed to prove
the treasonous intent of Messrs. Burr and
Wilkinson and their agents, Frederick

Bates and James Neelly. But more
importantly, I enclose a chalice discovered
in the river that bears your name, at the
headwaters of the Missouri, which laid
buried in silt and which ultimately led me
to a discovery of unbelievable proportions.

My discovery began when I climbed
a cylindrical rock that allowed me a total
view of the large mesa known as Fort Rock.
I could see what others did not and what the
chalice I had found truly meant. Climbing
to the summit of the mesa, I searched and
searched but could not find an entranceway.

Calamity almost ensued as I was
ready to give up my quest when I walked to
the edge of the mesa and looked all around
me at the wonders of the land before me and
looked at the rivers that lay below me, and
I imagined them as how they had looked
hundreds of years before, and then the
answer came to me.

Concerned greatly with the security
of this correspondence reaching your hands,
and yours alone, I will not detail that insight
and will leave it to you to further explore
and discover my meaning. But understand
that the golden chalice I send to you and

the contents of the leather pouch are merely
a small sample of what I provide my nation as
my last bequest.

Your most trusted servant,
Meriwether Lewis"

A gust of wind and a flicker of the candlelight ended his trance. The fever was playing tricks with him, and he was concerned that he had not given enough information, but his paranoia concerning his circumstances would not allow him to do so. He placed the letter in a leather satchel, along with a leather pouch, other pieces of correspondence, and the chalice he had wrapped in deerskin, and summoned his servant, John Pearny, who entered the cabin.

Pearny held his hat in his hand and his body shook as the shadows cast by the moving flame of the candle illuminated the visage of his master and, as Pearny listed to his instructions, he could only assume that it was the visage of a madman.

Pearny was quick to exit the cabin and did not look back. He mounted his horse and headed west and took the next fork off the Trace, southwest to the Mississippi. There he took money from a small leather pouch filled with coins that his master had given him and bought passage to New Orleans, and then passage by boat to Washington, D.C., where he had been instructed to give the contents of the leather satchel to no one but Jefferson.

Back at the cabin, the great Meriwether Lewis stood in the doorway to watch his servant leave, and when he was gone, looked at the sky and knew that it was only a few hours until dawn. He sighed with resignation, knowing that he would never see its arrival.

MONTICELLO CHARLOTTESVILLE, VIRGINIA

SPRING 1810

CHAPTER 3

Thomas Jefferson sat in his study, at his desk, covered with paper, an open leather satchel lying beside his chair. He affixed reading glasses to the bridge of his nose and stared at the object that had been wrapped in deerskin and occupied a corner of the desk and then returned his attention to the correspondence that he was once again reviewing, a letter from James Neelly dated 18 October 1809, informing him of the death of Meriwether Lewis. It would appear to be an apparent suicide. The letter described a man who was in the midst of losing his mind. He had confirmed Neelly's story with other sources in the territory. Lewis was facing bankruptcy, his administration of the Territory had deteriorated, along with his person, and suicide did not seem an unrealistic end for such a man.

Then he glanced at the leather satchel at his feet and picked up another stack of papers . . . papers and a letter from Lewis provided him by John Pearny, along with the chalice and the contents of a leather pouch. Pearny had also composed his own letter requesting payment for service to Governor Lewis for which he had not yet been paid.

Jefferson took off his glasses and slumped back in his chair.

"Poor Pearny. Were you the messenger bringing news of one of the most amazing discoveries in the history of the world, or were you only carrying the words of a madman?"

It was only two days ago, May 5th, when he received word from John Süverman that Pearny himself had passed. He arose and walked to the corner of the desk and picked up the object that had been wrapped in deerskin and stared at it.

"If Lewis was, indeed, insane and suicidal, *what* do I make of you?"

He walked over to the full-length window and stared out at the garden. The land was turning green.

"*A season of new birth,*" he thought. "*Is it really out there?*" he wondered, "*far to the west? A fantastic discovery that could help the continuance of the birth of this new nation . . . or is it merely the rantings of a madman?*"

He stared long and hard, deep in thought, and as usual, came to a rational decision as to what he must do. He turned and walked back to his desk, calling out as he did, "Burwell!"

His personal valet, Burwell Colbert, was not far away and appeared at once.

"Burwell, please, send word to Major Henry, if you would, and summon him to Monticello."

"As you wish, sir," said Burwell, and hurried out upon his task.

CHAPTER 4

Major Andrew Henry had been born in Fayette County, Pennsylvania. He was tall and slender with dark wavy hair and deep blue eyes. He was one of former president Thomas Jefferson's special agents. His reputation for being honest to a fault had preceded him and had served him well in his dealings with the President.

He had explored the upper Spanish Louisiana Territory, even before the Purchase went through, and had become interested in lead mining, and only last year had joined with Manuel Lisa and others to found the Missouri Fur Company.

Now pacing back and forth in Thomas Jefferson's study as Jefferson watched him from behind his desk, Henry said, "Just so I understand, Mr. President, you want me to travel back to the Three Forks of the Missouri and examine what we call 'Fort Rock', the large mesa that sits amid the three rivers, to see if I can discover an opening that would lead to some type of entrance into the mesa itself?"

Jefferson stood up and moved toward him.

"I know it's an unusual request, Major, but I have received information that such a possibility exists, and while I am not sure whether or not I believe it, I don't want to dismiss it out of hand, and I would like the matter investigated further."

He turned and walked back to his desk and stood at his chair.

"Major, you know I have made many requests of you. I presume you can develop a pretext for such a mission and conduct such an examination in secrecy and then report your findings back only to me?"

"Your excellency, you know I will do whatever you ask of me, even though I must admit I find this a particularly unusual assignment."

To Jefferson, the matter was settled and he sat down.

"I thank you, Major. I must make my own arrangements concerning this matter here in Virginia, and I am in the process of doing so."

"I would advise you that time is of the essence." And with that, he went back to his paperwork.

Major Henry knew when he had been dismissed.

"I will leave immediately, sir, and have my report back to you as soon as possible."

Jefferson never looked up.

"Thank you, Major," and the meeting was over.

FORT HENRY, THREE FORKS OF THE MISSOURI

SPRING 1810

CHAPTER 5

Major Andrew Henry summoned a dispatch rider into his quarters inside Fort Henry, which they had just completed above the confluence of the Jefferson and Madison Rivers.

They had survived another attack by the Blackfeet, although they had lost five and some horses, guns, ammunition, traps, and furs – and he was determined to lead his men back to St. Louis. He had done as Jefferson had asked, a fool's quest that had led to nothing, except to create more difficulty with the Blackfeet, but he had kept his passions in check as he had penned his letter, and he was now ready to send it by dispatch to the former President.

"To His Excellency, President Jefferson,

As you had requested, I conducted a thorough investigation of the area we had discussed and can find nothing that would lead me to further exploration. If you require me to take further action, please contact me in St. Louis, as attacks by the native tribes are continuing and I must lead my men back to safety.

Your humble servant,
Major Andrew Henry"

As the rider rode out of the gate with just enough light from early dawn to outline him against the sky as he headed toward the Missouri, Henry climbed one of the wooden ladders to the rampart and looked out over the fort's walls and watched the rider disappear into the surrounding timber.

He turned to head back down the ladder, but before he did, he looked around at the unimaginable beauty of dawn as it broke on this amazing frontier.

Then his gaze fell upon a Blackfoot arrow still sticking in the log wall of the fort and he looked back in the direction the rider had gone and hoped his message would get to Jefferson and not be lost forever in an Indian ambush or one of the many other dangers the beauty of the frontier concealed.

MONTICELLO, CHARLOTTESVILLE, VIRGINIA

JULY 4, 1826

CHAPTER 6

Thomas Jefferson was dying. Word had already been received that the same fate awaited John Adams, and there was much talk of divine providence that the two giants of the American Revolution would both expire fifty years to the day after the signing of the Declaration of Independence.

But Thomas Jefferson's mind was on other things as he contemplated the end. As often happens as one nears death, the many achievements he had accomplished in his lifetime, achievements that would forever make him a giant in the history of man, paled in comparison to the worries he held about what he had not achieved.

After saying goodbye to most of his family and staff, he asked that only his faithful servant, his personal valet, Burwell Colbert, remain.

Burwell approached as Jefferson motioned with his hand and handed him a letter.

"These are your letters of freedom, Burwell. You are now a free man, even though I have always considered you as such, as well as a friend and faithful confidant."

Burwell did not know how to thank him.

"The honor has been mine."

"Enough . . . enough, Burwell. We have other things to discuss, and I fear I do not have enough time.

In the secret compartment in my study, you will find a wooden box and a leather satchel containing documents. I want you to take these items to the vault at my retreat, deposit them inside, lock the entry, and then take the necessary steps to conceal it.

We will leave these items to history and the determination of a higher power as to whether or not they be found and, if so, hope that our countrymen have the combined wisdom to use them for the public good.

Promise me you will not fail in this, Burwell."

"You have my word, Mr. President," said Burwell, tears coming to his eyes.

"Good. Now go. Complete this last task for me, and then enjoy the benefits of a free man."

Burwell Colbert rose to his feet by the bed, unclasped the dying hand of his former owner and the man in the world he most admired and went to complete his final task, as he had promised.

Thomas Jefferson laid his head back on his pillow and closed his eyes. He had wrestled long and hard with what to do. It appeared from Henry's report and the reports he obtained from others that Lewis's words had indeed been those of a madman, but, inquisitive as he was, he could come up with no answer for the chalice and the contents of the leather pouch.

In the end, it was his misgivings about what his country would do with the discovery, if it really did exist, that led him to his decision and his hope that it would be found by wise and prudent men.

MIAMI, FLORIDA

PRESENT DAY

CHAPTER 7

Jake was still upset as he rubbed the back of his neck where the barrel of a weapon held by the man sitting across from him had been placed. He stared long and hard at a black man, middle aged, physically fit, obviously having no idea what to do next.

"You know, that little stunt of yours could have gotten you killed," said Jake.

"Mr. Sullivan, I know. I explained myself to you, and I apologized. I'm asking you to hear me out. If you want me to leave . . . if you want to have me arrested . . . do it. Otherwise, just listen."

Despite his anger, Jake was intrigued . . . intrigued as to why a man would go to such lengths just to tell him his story, and he sat back in his chair.

"Go ahead," said Jake, "but make it quick . . . and it better be good."

"My name is Adam Colbert. My great-great-grandfather was a man named Burwell Colbert. He was the personal valet of Thomas Jefferson. When Mr. Jefferson died, he gave my great- great-granddaddy his freedom, and he got a job working as a painter at the University of Virginia."

"There is more to this story, isn't there?" said Jake.

"Just be patient, Mr. Sullivan. Through a whole series of events that don't matter much, I became a maintenance worker at the University. Me and my family live in Charlottesville."

"So you're telling me you came the whole way from Charlottesville to meet with me?"

"Told you, Mr. Sullivan, I tried to get in touch with you, but that didn't seem to work, so I didn't have much choice. Now, as I was sayin', I worked as a maintenance man. We had a pipe bust and we had to tear out a section of wall in one of the older sections, and I found, wrapped in an oil skin . . . this," and he held up what appeared to be a small book bound in leather.

"And that is?" asked Jake.

"This is the diary of Burwell Colbert, and I want you to read the entry for July 4, 1826."

"*Almighty God looked down on Mr. Jefferson and carried him into the heavens. Fifty years to the day from when this country became free, and today I become free. My master gave me one last task to perform before I join the ranks of free men, and perform it I did. I was sworn to secrecy and Mr. Jefferson believed these matters should be in the hand of a divine providence as to whether anyone else ever learns of it. But after thinking about what I did, I think divine providence might need a helping hand. Mr. Jefferson had me put a leather satchel containing many papers and an item wrapped in deerskin in a box in a secret vault that I had created for him and that only he and I knew of. I had seen the item before sitting on a corner of his desk when I was doing work in his study.*"

The item was a gold chalice with funny markings I could not recognize and held what seemed to me to be precious gems of some kind. As I placed the items in the vault as I was told by Mr. Jefferson, my curiosity got the best of me and I looked into the satchel and tried to make out the words on the papers it contained. While I have some reading and writing skills, they are limited, but I did recognize the signature on at least one of the letters being that of Mr. Lewis, whom I had met during one of his meetings with Mr. Jefferson. The papers tell about some type of discovery and I can only think it has something to do with the chalice, but it is for others with far greater skills than me to find out. Whoever finds this diary can follow the clue I leave behind."

And then there was a drawing.

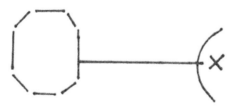

"Okay, Mr. Colbert. I've read it. What exactly do you think this is?"

"I thought about it long and hard, Mr. Sullivan, and I think the explorer, Meriwether Lewis, found some type of gold chalice during the course of his exploring, filled with precious gems, and sent it to Jefferson."

It was obvious that Colbert had paused for dramatic effect.

"Fine," said Jake, "what are you trying to get at?"

"Simple. I think that Lewis, during his expeditions, found Cibola."

"Cibola?"

"Yeah . . . Cibola . . . the Seven Cities of Gold."

"And you're getting all that from an entry in your great- great-grandfather's diary?"

"Yeah, look, man . . . he left a clue . . . thought it might be important. I put it together. I've been doing some reading. A lot of people think that Cibola exists somewhere out west. What if Lewis found it and told Jefferson about it?"

"If that's true, why wouldn't Jefferson have sent out somebody to bring back the treasure?"

"I don't know. Maybe he thought there was no one he could trust. Maybe he thought the country wasn't ready yet. I don't know. He seems to have hidden everything . . . thinking it might be found by somebody later. I don't know. I just think there is something to it."

Jake suddenly realized where this was going.

"And you brought it to me because . . ."

"'Cause I've read about you in the papers . . . that treasure down in Cuba . . . you found the one in Jamaica . . . I mean, hell, if anybody can find it, you can."

"You do know I'm a federal prosecutor?"

"Yeah . . . I mean I know your day job is a prosecutor, but you sure as hell seem to find a lot of treasure."

Jake leaned up onto his elbows on his desk and rubbed his eyes and then muttered under his breath, "Goddamn papers."

He looked up and said, "Look, Mr. Colbert, when 'we' . . . and I do say 'we' because it wasn't just me who found what you're referring to . . . that was because when we found these things the government was involved in doing other things, okay? We didn't go out just to find secret treasure. It just so happened we got lucky and found . . . some things we hadn't planned on. Unfortunately, I can't tell you any more than that, but trust me when I tell you that this isn't something that I . . ."

"But look . . . Mr. Sullivan, this has important ramifications for the country. I mean, if this is true, just think . . . man . . . maybe we can pay off the national debt . . . help people . . . you know . . . I don't know, but there's something here . . . and it involves history . . . Lewis and Jefferson. Don't you want to get to the bottom of it?"

Jake leaned back in his chair and put his hands up.

"You want this to be a real life repeat of the movie 'National Treasure' . . . but that was just a movie.

Look, I'm sorry, Mr. Colbert, but like I told you, I am not a treasure hunter. I can't just leave my job and go look for treasure somewhere out west. Look, think how long these things would have been around. Surely someone would have found them, don't you think?"

"You need to do some readin' Mr. Sullivan. There's a lot of these things out in the world that people have been looking after for years and no one's ever found them . . . and then, all of a sudden . . . they do. I read about that guy down in Key West. Man, he spent his whole life looking for that treasure out in the Gulf . . . but he found it . . . after years of looking, he found it."

Jake knew he was talking about Mel Fisher and the gold from the *Atocha*.

"Yes, he did. You're right. But he was a treasure hunter. That's what he did . . . that's all he did. I'm not. That's the difference. Maybe you can find someone who'd be interested in doing this," and then Jake's eyes narrowed and he looked long and hard at Mr. Colbert. "Tell me . . . what do you want out of this?"

"I don't know . . . maybe . . . you know . . . if it's found . . . I could get a finder's fee or something."

"I see."

Colbert lowered his head. His hands were in his lap, and he started to wring them. Then he looked back up at Jake Sullivan.

"All right, Mr. Sullivan, you want the truth? I'll give you the truth. I have a granddaughter . . . the only grandchild I have . . . the joy of my life. She has a very severe case of one of those crazy diseases I can't even pronounce. She's only three years old. They say she'll never see six. There is a program she could get into. Might help her . . . might not . . . but it gives her a chance . . . and it costs a lot of money . . . money that I don't have and nobody I know has. I don't want a dime, Mr. Sullivan, not a Goddamn dime . . . but I do want to give that little baby girl a chance . . . and all I want is enough to get her in that program to give her that chance. That's all."

Jake could see he was telling the truth and he softened his tone.

"I'm sorry about your granddaughter, I truly am, and I wish I could help you, but I just can't. This isn't something that I can get involved in. I'm sorry."

Colbert sighed with the realization that their talk was over. Then he brought his hands down on top of his thighs.

"Okay. What happens now? You gonna call the cops? What?"

"No. I'm not going to do anything. I'm going to give you back your diary and I'm going to wish you luck . . . both you and your granddaughter . . . then I'm going to walk you to the elevator and say goodnight. C'mon, let's go," and he went to get up out of his seat.

Colbert stood also and said, "Yeah, luck . . . that's what I need . . . luck. I've taken up enough of your time, Mr. Sullivan. I know where the elevator is. I promise, I'll get on it and I'll be gone," and he headed for the door, but then stopped and turned. "And again, I'm sorry about the gun thing. Desperate men do desperate things. All I wanted to do was talk to you," and he walked out before Jake could say anything.

Jake sat back at his desk and heard the elevator door close. He got out a piece of paper and drew the strange design he had seen in the diary of Burwell Colbert.

CHAPTER 8

It was mid-morning two weeks after Jake's late night visitor. He and Mike were sitting in the office, with Jake going over some paper-work and Mike reading the morning paper. It had been slow the last week or so, but a major sting had just been approved for the Port of Miami. Some chatter had been picked up about contraband coming into the country through some bad guys known to be associated with terrorist organizations, and the threat level had been heightened in the Miami area.

Jake had just been reading the final details of a report on the matter.

"Looks like we're going to get busy. This thing down at the port might be the real deal."

Mike looked up from his newspaper.

"Well, let's hope it's just a bunch of noise, like usual. However, reading the good old Metro section . . . it appears that one of our favorite congressmen got himself involved in a little mess . . . appears some improper funds changed hands. Isn't this the same guy, one of those jerks that tried to vote down our funding?" and he folded the paper and handed it to Jake.

As Jake unfolded the paper and scanned the article, he started to smile, when his eyes caught a smaller headline.

"Holy shit!"

"What are you surprised for? We knew that guy was no good."

"That's not what I'm talking about. It's Adam Colbert. His body was just washed ashore." He looked up at Mike. "He was beaten to death and apparently tortured." Jake then got up and walked to the windows and stared out at the Atlantic.

"Who the hell is Adam Colbert?" asked Mike.

"A long story," said Jake.

"It's not like I don't have time," Mike replied.

"Yeah, I guess you're right," and Jake proceeded to tell him the story of his late night visitor.

CHAPTER 9

"So this guy who turned up on the beach, put a gun to the back of your head, and told you some crazy story about a lost city of gold that involves Meriwether Lewis, Thomas Jefferson, and a distant relative . . . and you never thought to tell me about it?"

"It was one of those things. The kids came down for a visit . . . we got busy here at the office. I felt bad for the guy, but I just let it go."

Mike held up the paper.

"And now you think this is no coincidence?"

"I don't know, Mike. I just have a lot of questions. Why did he stay here in Miami? Why didn't he go back home to Charlottesville?"

Just then, Eva came in and knocked on the door jam.

"There's someone here to see you, Jake . . . a lady by the name of Nina Colbert."

Jake and Mike exchanged glances and Jake said, "Send her in."

Jake approached the small black woman and held out his hand.

"Mrs. Colbert, I'm Jake Sullivan. Please have a seat," and he directed her to a chair.

"Mr. Sullivan, my name is Nina Colbert. I'm Adam Colbert's wife."

"This is Mike Lang, my investigator, Mrs. Colbert. He and I just read about Adam in the paper. We're so sorry for your loss."

Jake could see a look he had seen on the faces of victims' relatives many times before . . . a look of fear, anger, sadness . . . but he also saw resolve in the face of Nina Colbert.

"I don't want you to be sorry, Mr. Sullivan. I want you to do something about it. My husband was a good man . . . and he came to you out of concern for our baby grandchild. He was so frustrated, Mr. Sullivan. He couldn't get to see you, and that's why he did what he did."

"He told you about that, I take it?" asked Jake.

"He did. He called me. He told me he had spoken with you, what he had done, and that he was coming home 'cause you were his last chance and you weren't going to do anything."

"I'm sorry, Mrs. Colbert, I truly am . . . but it just wasn't something I could do. But let me ask you . . . did Adam come home?"

"No. He called me the next morning and said he had met somebody who was willing to help him and he was going to meet with his partners that day . . . and that was the last I ever heard from him . . . until I got a call from your coroner's office down here," and she started to cry. "They got his information from his wallet and . . ." she turned her head away, taking a handkerchief out of her purse, and began to wipe her eyes.

Jake went over and knelt beside the chair.

"Take your time, Mrs. Colbert. I know this must be very hard for you. Look, let me see what I can do. I'll talk to the local authorities and see what I can find out."

"You don't have to find out nothin', Mr. Sullivan!" Mrs. Colbert said angrily, starting to rise. "My husband was tortured . . . beaten . . . killed. You think that has no connection to what he told you? You want to do something for me? You want to do something for my husband? You want to do something for our grandchild? Do what Adam asked you to do! Find out what all this means! Make sure my husband didn't die for nothin'!"

Jake got up and turned to walk toward the window. Mike looked at him and just shook his head and smiled and then got up and walked over to Mrs. Colbert, who was now standing, and took her hand.

"Mrs. Colbert, we'll look into this . . . the whole thing . . . and we'll see what we can find out."

"Thank you, Mr. Lang," and she looked toward Jake. "Mr. Sullivan?" she asked.

After a few seconds, Jake turned, his hands on his hips, and looked at Mike, who was still smiling, and then looked at her and shook his head.

"You heard him, Mrs. Colbert. We'll look into it. We'll see what we can do."

"Thank you. Thank you both," and she seemed to steel herself. "Now, I have to go identify my husband and say goodbye, and then I have to get back to Charlottesville. Please keep me informed."

"We will," said Jake, "I promise."

"Thank you again," she said to both of them, and then turned and went out the door.

Jake looked at Mike.

"Really?" he said.

"Oh, c'mon, Jake. You knew you were going to do it."

"Oh? And how do you know that?" said Jake.

"Because . . . the only reason he was killed was because he met with you . . . and you're not going to let that go."

CHAPTER 10

Jake picked up the phone and pressed the button.

"Eva, do a little research and find me the top guy with knowledge of Thomas Jefferson. Yes, we are going to try to help her. Yes . . . yes . . . Eva, just find the guy, okay?"

Mike was sitting across the desk and started laughing.

"I take it Eva's happy we're helping the lady?" he asked.

"Of course," said Jake. "Now, c'mon. Let's get to work while she's getting into this. We've got to get this dock thing set up."

Less than an hour later Eva again knocked on the entrance to Jake's office.

"What's up, Eva?" he asked.

She walked over and handed him a slip of paper.

"This appears to be the guy. If you want to know anything about Thomas Jefferson, that's who to ask."

"Thanks, Eva."

Just then, Mike hung up the phone.

"I talked to a friend of mine in the homicide division at Miami-Dade. Looks like our friend was really worked over . . . burns, cuts . . . really brutal. He had his wallet and a couple bucks on him, but nothing with any papers."

Jake swiveled in his chair and tented his hands in front of him.

"I didn't think there would be. If his death was tied into his meeting with me, whoever killed him took the diary."

"So what are you going to tell the Jefferson hotshot? We don't have anything!"

Jake turned and held up a piece of paper.

"I have this. I made a sketch of the clue that Colbert's great-great-grandfather put in the letter he showed me," and he handed it to Mike.

"What is this thing? Some kind of instrument? A mechanism of some kind?"

"I don't have a clue," said Jake.

"You heard back from this guy at UVA yet?" asked Mike.

"Not yet," and he picked up a pile of paperwork. "Regarding other things, how are we doing on the Port of Miami?"

"Everything's coming into place. We should be ready."

"Good. I have a bad feeling about this one."

"You need to get your mind off it for a while. Let's go see Larry. Maybe he can add some information."

CHAPTER 11

It was a beautiful day in Miami as they headed out to No. 1 Bob Hope Road, the Miami-Dade County Medical Examiner's Office.

They parked and went inside, expecting to hear the newest "Gulf Western" or "Trop Rock" along with the ever-present Jimmy Buffett songs that made up the ongoing playlist of Larry Hussey, Chief Medical Examiner, but the office was strangely quiet.

After they announced the reason for their visit to the receptionist, they sat and waited until a young lady dressed in a white lab coat came out to meet them.

"Mr. Sullivan . . . Mr. Lang . . . I'm Mitzie Burke, Associate Medical Examiner," and she held out her hand to each of them.

Jake took her hand and introduced them.

"Ms. Burke, I'm Jake Sullivan, and this is my investigator, Mike Lang."

"Oh, I definitely know who you are, Mr. Sullivan, and also you, Mr. Lang. Dr. Hussey has spent many hours regaling me with tales of your exploits."

"Don't believe everything old Larry tells you," said Mike. "He gets carried away at times, Ms. Burke."

She was tall, with auburn hair that framed a long face, with extremely beautiful eyes, alive with mischief, behind a pair of round, tortoiseshell framed glasses.

"That's Dr. Burke," she said, looking at Mike and then at Jake, "and Dr. Hussey has assured me that his tales are absolutely true. Now, gentlemen, how may I help you?"

"We'd like to see Adam Colbert's body, if we may," said Jake, hoping to smooth over their error in not referring to her in her professional capacity.

She turned quickly on her heel.

"A horrible thing, that one," she said. "Please follow me," as she headed toward a set of stainless steel doors with small glass windows at the top.

Based on their too many visits to this office, they followed along and readied themselves to see the body of another victim.

"Adam Colbert . . . vault number 14," said Dr. Burke as she bent down to open the drawer, pull out the body, and pulled back the sheet. The body had been cleaned, but the bruising and burn marks were still evident on the face and torso.

"Looks like someone really put him through it," said Jake.

"Yeah, someone who likes it," said Mike.

"This isn't the worst of it," she said, holding up Mr. Colbert's right hand.

Jake and Mike both grimaced as they saw that two fingers had been snipped off.

"Poor guy," said Mike, "he must have started talking after the second one."

"Yeah . . . either that, or they realized he had nothing to tell them."

"He's lucky," said Dr. Burke.

"How so?" asked Jake.

"He had a heart attack . . . probably brought on by the torture. But these bastards would've kept going if he hadn't died on them."

"Thanks, Dr. Burke," said Jake, as she recovered the body with the sheet, rolled the drawer into the vault, and closed the metallic door so that it latched.

"Anything else you can tell us about this, Doc?" asked Mike.

"Not really. Obviously, some sadist wanted something from the poor man, but I can't tell you whether they got it or not."

"It's my understanding there was nothing of interest found with the body," said Jake. "We are looking for a small leather book."

Dr. Burke moved to a wall, along which hung several clipboards. She picked up one and looked at it.

"No, nothing like that. Only a watch, wedding band, a cell phone, and car keys. We gave all of it to his wife when she came in and identified the body."

"I'll go call Eva," said Mike, "and have her call Mrs. Colbert and see if she was able to locate the car and where he had been staying, and I'll get a team to check it out."

"Good. And get a subpoena for his phone records," said Jake. "Thanks, Mike."

"Nice meeting you, Dr. Burke," said Mike as he exited.

"Same to you, Mr. Lang," she said, and then looked at Jake.

"Anything else I can do for you, Mr. Sullivan?"

"No. Thank you Doctor, I appreciate it. So, how are you and Larry getting along?"

"Very well, why do you ask?"

"Well, Larry's a good ole' boy from outside of Lubbock, Texas, and you seem . . . I don't know . . ."

"A bit more proper," she interjected, smiling.

"Yeah, something like that," said Jake.

"Mr. Sullivan, given what Dr. Hussey has told me, I don't think you're a person that takes things at face value."

"No, no . . . I apologize. I didn't mean anything by . . ." and she cut him off again.

"No need for apologies. Let me put it to you this way . . . Dr. Hussey did his undergrad at Texas Tech and is a big fan of the football team. The team he really dislikes . . . Texas A & M. Guess where I went? It took a long night and several rounds of tequila to prove to him it was worth his while to hire me as his assistant."

"So you're . . . ?"

"You got it, Mr. Sullivan. Texan born and bred. Hell, I'm even making in-roads onto his playlist."

Jake laughed.

"Well, then you are obviously the proper selection."

"We shall see, Mr. Sullivan . . . we shall see."

"Well, it's been a pleasure, Dr. Burke, and I thank you again for your time," and he started to leave when she called after him.

"Mr. Sullivan . . ."

"Yes, ma'am?" he said.

"I hope you catch the guys who did this. These are some bad people."

"I have a feeling I know who they belong to. You're right, they are bad people," and with that, he was gone.

CHAPTER 12

It wasn't until the next day that Jake received a call from David Harper, Professor Emeritus at the University of Virginia and head of Jefferson Studies.

"Dr. Harper, thanks for calling me back. I appreciate it," said Jake. "You're on speaker. My investigator, Mike Lang, is here in the office with me."

"Mr. Sullivan . . . Mr. Lang . . . I must admit, I was somewhat curious when I received your message. What does a Miami Federal Prosecutor and his investigator want to do with me?"

"Oh, it's nothing like that, Dr. Harper. We received some information from a gentleman who was, unfortunately, murdered after we received that information, and it has something to do with some historical references involving Thomas Jefferson, and I wanted to see if we could come up and visit you and pick your brain a little."

"You think this might have something to do with this man's murder?"

"It appears that way, but that's what we want to find out. We want to see if you can give us some insight into the information this gentleman provided."

"What's the information?"

"I'd rather not discuss that over the phone, if you don't mind."

"Well, sure, I can make some time for you. How about, uh . . . let me look at my calendar . . . how about, uh, day after tomorrow?"

Jake looked at Mike and Mike shook his head affirmatively.

"Yeah, looks like we should have everything we're working on here on some other matters tied up so that we can get away for a day. Mike and I will see you then."

"Good." said Dr. Harper, "Now I'm curious," and the line went dead.

"All right," said Jake, "that gives us today and tomorrow to get this sting set up and ready to roll. I want it done before we leave."

"You got it," said Mike, heading out the door.

UNIVERSITY OF VIRGINIA CHARLOTTESVILLE, VIRGINIA

CHAPTER 13

Jake and Mike were ushered into Professor Harper's office at the University of Virginia and they introduced themselves.

"So, gentlemen," said Dr. Harper, taking a seat behind his desk, "what is this all about?"

Jake proceeded to tell him about the diary from Burwell Colbert that was found at the University.

"And you have no idea where this diary is?" asked Harper.

"I'm afraid not. It wasn't recovered with the body, and we're assuming that whoever killed Mr. Colbert took it."

"What a tragedy," said Harper, shaking his head.

"Yeah, he appeared to be a pretty decent man."

"Oh, yes, of course . . . Mr. Colbert. I'm sorry. I was talking about the diary. What a historical find this would be for Jefferson scholars. Burwell Colbert was Jefferson's personal valet and privy to probably everything important that happened during Jefferson's presidency and thereafter. It would have made for fascinating reading. But, gentlemen, I'm sorry . . . if that's all you have, I don't see what you need from me."

"Well, as I told you, Burwell referred to some type of secret vault, and I know you're an expert on Monticello. Have you discovered anything like that? Have you heard of anything like that? Any place where we could begin to look?"

Harper sat back in his chair and smiled.

"No, I'm afraid not, Mr. Sullivan. There have been countless stories about Monticello and secret passages and secret rooms, but believe me, that building has been analyzed every way possible. It's been gone over inside and out. It's been x-rayed, sonar has been used . . . every device we have available to search for historical artifacts . . . and we've never discovered anything other than what was shown in Jefferson's architectural drawings before it was built . . . and what could be seen with the naked eye."

"That's sort of what I thought, but I wanted to ask you before I showed you this. Burwell Colbert said he was leaving a clue at the end of his diary entry and I made a sketch of his drawing, and this is what it looks like," and he handed the sketch to Dr. Harper.

Harper stared at it and shook his head.

"I can't say I've seen anything like this at Monticello. It doesn't look like . . ." and he stopped.

"What is it?" asked Jake.

Harper looked up and smiled.

"I think the problem, gentlemen, is that we're talking about the wrong house."

"What do you mean the wrong house?" asked Mike.

"If you asked anyone in the United States with any knowledge of history as to what was Thomas Jefferson's favorite Virginia retreat where he went when he wanted to get away from everything, 99.9% would give the answer 'Monticello,' but they would all be wrong. Monticello was Thomas Jefferson's formal home where he entertained guests, including heads of state, famous artists, scientists, and other people of stature. You have to realize that after the United States was founded, when anyone of significance came to this country, they all went to see Thomas Jefferson, and Monticello was the house where those events took place, but when Thomas Jefferson wanted to get away to write, to read, to conduct experiments, or to simply be by himself, tending to his crops and his gardens . . . he didn't go to Monticello. He built another home for himself in Lynchburg, Virginia . . . another estate, called Poplar Forest. This drawing is an outline of the buildings at that location. This 'x' is on a mounded hillside where this long row of offices abruptly ends."

"This place still exist?" asked Jake. "I've never heard of it."

"As I said, everyone concentrates on Monticello, but yes, it still exists. It's run by The Corporation For Jefferson's Poplar Forest, an entity that takes care of it, runs it, and maintains it," and he sat back in his chair, rubbing his chin, looking at the drawing. "And you know, it makes sense."

"What do you mean?" asked Mike.

"Well, if there was a secret vault anywhere where Jefferson would want to keep things important to him, it wouldn't be at Monticello. He was smart enough to realize his place in history. He knew that it would become some type of landmark . . . but the smaller home that no one knows about . . . might be a good place to keep things. The only thing that concerns me," Harper went on, "is that the octagonal main house here," he said, pointing to the drawing, "has always existed, but the rectangular walkway that housed offices was destroyed. Its foundation was discovered, and it was reconstructed, and I have to think that surely during that reconstruction any vault or opening to a vault would have been found."

"Wait a minute . . . one thing bothers me," said Jake, "wasn't Burwell Colbert, Jefferson's personal valet, just at Monticello?"

"No, not at all," said Harper. "The record is very clear that Burwell Colbert also oversaw a great deal of the work at Poplar Forest . . . even when it was being built."

"I just thought of something," said Mike, "when did work begin on this house?"

"It was started in 1806 ... that is, the main house. This rectagonal wing was completed around 1814. We're not exactly sure when it began, but it was probably somewhere around 1810 or 1811. Why do you ask?"

"What if ... what was the wing used for?" asked Mike.

"It was basically for the servants to conduct the daily business of the house ... cooking, building, and doing things that needed done to maintain the place."

"Do you think it could be possible that it was built because of something that Jefferson learned? To provide him a way to get from a secret vault at the far end to his actual home?"

Harper shook his head.

"Anything is possible, Mr. Lang. Certainly, there's never been anything until now to suggest that would be a possibility, but, quite frankly, if you're giving an accurate description of what was in Burwell Colbert's diary, there is a vault on that property ... and if located where he says, that certainly could have been one of the reasons."

"Let me ask you something," said Jake, "how much difficulty are we going to have to get in there to do some digging?"

Harper sighed and said, "That could be a problem. People are very, very concerned about these venues and their historical significance. I know that's true about Monticello, and it's also true about the house in Lynchburg. I think it can be done, but I think you're going to have to have some pretty good authority behind you to get it done."

Jake looked at Mike and smiled.

"I think we might be able to get that, Dr. Harper," and he stood up. "We'll work on that, and I wonder if you can do some preliminary work with the folks at Poplar Forest ... sort of let them know what we're looking for and why?"

"Yeah, sure, I'd be happy to ... on one condition ..."

"What's that?" asked Jake.

"That anything we find becomes part of the artifacts of Thomas Jefferson and is preserved as agreed to between the folks at Poplar Forest and the folks here at the Jefferson Foundation."

"I don't think that will be a problem, Dr. Harper," said Jake. "We need to see what's there first, but we understand we're dealing with a moment in history . . . and we also understand the significance of that."

"That's good enough for me," said Harper. "The reputations of you two gentlemen precede you. I know what you've done in other situations. I'll get on the phone and make some calls and then make a personal visit to Poplar Forest."

"After we get the authority we might need to do this, we'll be back in touch," said Jake to Harper, who was already on the phone and waving them out of the office.

THE WHITE HOUSE
WASHINGTON,
D.C.

CHAPTER 14

Jake and Mike spent the night in Charlottesville and then drove to D.C. the next morning.

"I don't have time for another treasure hunt," said Jason Bates, "not with everything else that is going on here . . . and even more importantly, with what's going on in Miami. I need you two down there doing your job to make sure whatever the hell they're sending our way doesn't get in. Look guys, this is the real deal. There hasn't been this much chatter since 9/11. Something big is being planned."

"I understand, Jason," said Jake, "and believe me, we've been working on nothing else for the past couple weeks. Everything is in place, and we're in continuous contact with everybody involved."

"Good!" said President Jordan's Chief of Staff, "because I think you're involved more than you know."

"What's that mean?" asked Mike.

"It means that the chatter about the Port of Miami isn't just accidental."

"And?" asked Jake.

Bates looked down at his desk.

"And . . . the chatter also indicates that Group 45 is involved."

"So you think Joan Taylor is behind this?" And she picked the Port of Miami because of me?"

"I can't rule it out," said Bates.

Mike looked up.

"You think this thing with Colbert was done by Group 45, don't you? You think they're doing this as a distraction to get us off our game? That bitch wants to bring that stuff in right under our noses."

"Again, Lang, I can't rule it out."

"Shit!" said Mike, looking away.

"What if it isn't a distraction?" asked Jake. "What if they're after it, too? You know, we've done some serious damage to their finances. Maybe they're looking for another source of income."

"Oh, c'mon Jake! You mean the Seven Cities of Gold? Cibola? Where was it the last time . . . in that movie . . . Mount Rushmore?"

"I know. I understand, Jason. And I'm not talking about launching a full-scale treasure hunt. All I want to do is get the authority from the White House to dig up a small space at Thomas Jefferson's house in Lynchburg, Virginia. It's not going to take any time away from our other duties, and after that, we can talk about the bigger picture."

"No, leave it go, Jake. He's probably right. It probably is a myth . . . just like Meyer Lansky's treasure in Cuba, and Henry Morgan's treasure in Jamaica, and . . ."

"Okay, Lang. I get it," said Bates. "I get it. I admit your track record is pretty good, and I suppose," he said, looking at Jake, "you've consulted your gut on this?"

"Let me put it this way," said Jake, "I don't think Burwell Colbert lied in his diary, and I don't think Adam Colbert's death was a coincidence or a distraction."

"Okay," said Bates, raising his hand in surrender as he sat heavily in his chair. "What do you want?"

"A directive with the full authority of the White House to take any and all necessary action in this matter."

"What's your next step?" asked Bates.

"Once we have the document in our hands," said Mike, "we'll call Professor Harper and set up a meeting at Poplar Forest in Lynchburg."

"All right," said Bates, standing. "Give me until the end of business. In the meantime, get down to the situation room and keep your eyes on the Port of Miami," and with that, he was gone.

"You heard the man," said Jake.

"You know," said Mike as they were leaving, "the funny thing is . . . I'm actually starting to like the guy."

POPLAR FOREST
LYNCHBURG, VIRGINIA

CHAPTER 15

Once the Presidential Directive had been received from Bates, Jake placed a call to Harper and made arrangements to meet with him and Edward Milton, the President of the Corporation For Jefferson's Poplar Forest.

They spent their night at the White House, most of it in the situation room, making sure everything was a go at the Port of Miami.

The drive to Lynchburg was uneventful, and as they entered the site, Harper and Milton were there to greet them.

After introductions, Milton took over the conversation. He was a small, balding man with wire-rimmed glasses set on his nose and a tweed jacket with a pipe protruding from the breast pocket . . . a stereotypical academician.

"Before we proceed, gentlemen, I have to tell you that I've consulted with other members of the Board, and we absolutely refuse to allow you or anyone else to do any digging on this property. It is ridiculous to believe that during the excavation that found the proper coordinates for the wing and its rebuilding, that we would have missed a vault of some kind beneath it. There are no secret passageways, vaults, or anything else here at Poplar Forest."

Jake took the document out of his pocket and handed it to Milton.

"You may be right, Mr. Milton, but, unfortunately, this is a matter of national security, and we have to make sure. You might want to read that directive."

Milton's whole posture seemed to sag as he read through the directive and realized that his lecture had been for naught and that an excavation would soon commence at Poplar Forest.

"We have a forensic team from Quantico on the way," said Mike, "and believe we can do this with as little damage as possible. All we're interested in is removing the floor of that wing right where it meets the mound at its end."

"Very well," said Milton, snapping off his words and thrusting the directive back at Jake. "But be advised that any damage to the historical nature of this property is fully your responsibility."

"Understood," said Jake. "Now, if you don't mind, we'd like to get busy."

Milton reluctantly directed them to the back wall of the wing and they stood upon rough floorboards created to meet the standards of Jefferson's time as best they could.

"I don't think that removing these floorboards will be too much of a problem," said Jake as he turned to Milton. "What was underneath this when the excavation was being done?"

"Just dirt."

"And to recreate this . . . was there a poured foundation put in place?"

"Yes, there was," said Milton.

"Then we're going to have to go through that, too."

"This is ridiculous!" said Milton as he stomped away.

"I don't think that guy like us," said Mike.

"You'll have to excuse him," said Harper. "We academics get a little frustrated when government steps in."

Just then a man approached them from the other end of the wing, with other men trailing behind him, all in work clothes, except for vests that spelled out "FBI" across the chest.

"Mr. Sullivan . . . Mr. Lang," he said, extending his hand. "I'm Agent Jim Hollister. We're here from the Forensic Unit at Quantico."

"Right this way, gentlemen. We'll tell you where to start."

Several hours had passed and Jake and Mike were waiting in a sitting area of the main house at Poplar Forest when Hollister approached them, his jeans dusty from his labors.

"I'm afraid we've struck out, gentlemen. We took out the floorboards, cracked open the cement, and dug down through the dirt until we hit solid stone. We can't seem to find any place where some type of trapdoor could exist."

"Mind if we take a look?" said Mike.

"Nope. Follow me," and Mike and Jake went out after Hollister.

When they got to the site, they saw that what Hollister had told them was correct. The floorboards had been removed and the concrete taken out in chunks, and there were barrels of earth sitting outside that had been removed and kept separate so they could be replaced. Milton was there, also, as they approached.

"I told you this was ridiculous! All this was for nothing!"

Neither Jake nor Mike responded, and Mike bent down to examine the stone. He hollered back without turning around.

"Mr. Milton! When the foundation of this structure was excavated, how far outside of its lines did you go?"

"We only went to the edge of the foundation that was found."

"I want to go outside," said Mike, and he headed for the door as everyone looked at each other.

Jake said, "C'mon . . . he's on to something."

Mike was down on his haunches again, looking at the exterior of the foundation. Then he got up and looked around the land as it stretched out before him.

"You know, driving here I noticed a lot of rock formations throughout the woods . . . stones probably brought down by a glacier."

"That's right," said Milton, "and?"

"And," said Mike, walking up to him, "if you look at the surface of what we found inside and the surface of the rocks in the woods, they look exactly alike. So what if this isn't a solid rock formation, but a rock that was moved here to cover something?"

He then turned to Hollister.

"Agent Hollister, dig outside the excavation. See if you find the edge for that rock. If I'm right, and if you do, dig around it so it can be pulled out," and with that, he headed back toward the main house, passing Milton again.

"Don't worry, Mr. Milton, when we're all done, we'll put it back."

Jake just shook his head and smiled and followed after him.

CHAPTER 16

The next time Hollister appeared, he came running in.

"You were right, Mr. Lang! We found it!"

Jake and Mike got up and followed him to the dig site. Outside they could see a large flat stone lying in the grass. That stone had covered a wooden trap door that they could now see below them, with rusted hinges and a rusted hasp and padlock.

The forensic team carefully removed the lock and the hinges and then slowly lifted the wooden door, which was made of heavy timber and stayed in one piece. Beneath it there appeared to be brick steps leading down. Using flashlights, Jake and Mike led the way.

The steps led into a tunnel which had been excavated enough for them to walk almost erect, and the tunnel opened into a brick-lined cavern, the walls covered with wooden shelving that appeared to hold various books and portfolios of papers.

They would later discover that the ingenious Jefferson had a pipe extended through the earth mound above the cavern he had created, up through a hollow tree that came out at the top, so that fresh air was available in the cavern. At the bottom, there was a damper to seal out moisture and airflow when not in use, so as to keep the items in the cavern from becoming damp or brittle. The mortared brick on walls, ceiling, and floor kept out moisture from the ground. There were sconces on the walls holding candles, and in the center was a wooden desk, and on that desk sat a large leather satchel and a wooden box.

"Agent," said Jake to Hollister, "we need this box opened."

Milton, who had followed them down, stammered from the background, "Please! Please! Carefully . . . carefully! This is an amazing discovery."

Jake looked at Mike and just shook his head and smiled.

"Don't worry, Mr. Milton," said Mike, "these boys have done pretty well so far, don't you think?"

"Yes, yes, of course," said Milton. "I was only . . ." and his words trailed off.

The forensic team opened the box with little damage and removed a deerskin wrapped object from its interior, along with a small leather pouch. They then took off the deerskin to reveal a chalice, which appeared to be made from gold, with various signs carved into it. They emptied the small pouch into the chalice and it was soon filled with what appeared to be emeralds, rubies, and other precious gems.

One of the agents opened the large leather satchel and looked inside.

"I think we better take this with us," he said. "There's a lot of paper in here. We want to be careful."

Milton couldn't help himself.

"Please! Please! That belongs to the Corporation and no harm can come to it."

Harper had had enough.

"Look, Milton! I'm tired of this! We all agreed how this was going to be handled and where these items would eventually go. Now quit your whining about everything and let these men get on with their work."

For once, Milton didn't know what to say and turned on his heels and went back the way they had come.

"Nice work, Doc," said Mike.

"It's guys like him that makes everyone think that we're all assholes, like him."

Jake turned to Agent Hollister.

"All right, Agent. Get your team in here. I'm sure everything needs taken back to the lab to be cataloged, but that chalice and what's in this portfolio has top priority. That's what we have to have examined first."

"Understood," said Hollister. "All right men . . . let's go," and they began setting up lights on tripods to light up the entire cavern and set up a computer to index what they were taking out.

One agent was assigned to put the contents back into the box and take it and the satchel immediately to the lab at Quantico with Jake and Mike. Before they left, they approached Dr. Harper.

"Doctor, thanks for all your help. We never would have found this without you," said Jake.

"Yeah, make sure these guys do their job right," said Mike.

"What do you mean?" asked Dr. Harper.

"Between you and us," said Jake, "what really got Milton so rattled was that we made sure you were placed in charge of this little endeavor."

"Yeah," said Mike, "I don't think he likes someone else being the boss on his turf."

Harper just started laughing.

"Thanks, gentlemen. I appreciate it . . . I think."

"Keep us posted," said Jake.

"You got it," said Harper.

And with that, they and the agent, who had placed the box and the satchel in a sealed container, headed out for the drive to Quantico.

FBI LAB SERVICES QUANTICO, VIRGINIA

CHAPTER 17

It took the forensic specialists two and a half days to empty the leather satchel, clean the chalice, and the gems. The papers, chalice, and gems were all put under special lighting, under glass, with a special gas pumped in as a preservative.

Jake and Mike had spent their days and nights waiting, being updated on the situation in Miami and also getting updates when possible from Hollister. Finally, he called them in for a meeting at his office and gave them copies of the documents that they had taken from the pouch.

"I know we're not privy to the whole situation here," said Hollister, "but I also know your reputations, and given what we've found, I have a feeling that the copy on top is what you're looking for. The rest of those documents deal with Meriwether Lewis's financial situation, letters about his death, and the actions of his servant, John Pearny. Here's a version of what we think happened."

"Go ahead and tell us," said Jake.

"Given that top document, it appears that Meriwether Lewis found something on a mesa near what is now Three Forks, Montana, where the Madison and Jefferson Rivers meet the Missouri at its headwaters. According to this, he made some type of amazing discovery there by being able to enter that mesa. That's what he reported in that top document, which is a letter to former President

Jefferson in 1809. Jefferson had one of his agents, a Major Andrew Henry, who was one of the founders of the Missouri Fur Company, go out and scout the site and see if he could find an entrance. There's also a letter there from Henry saying he could not. It looks like that satchel that contained all these documents and the chalice and gems were brought back by Meriwether Lewis's servant, John Pearny, and delivered to Jefferson. The rest of that correspondence deals with what appears to be a plot by a group of co-conspirators led by Aaron Burr and a guy named Wilkinson, along with their subordinates named Neelly and Bates, to set up their own country with the help of Spain in the Louisiana Territory. Lewis discovered more of the gold and gems he sent back. I think he was very, very careful not to reveal how he actually discovered them for fear that the conspirators could also make the discovery and use whatever was there to finance their plot. But it looks like Jefferson agreed with this Neelly character, who wrote a letter describing Lewis's state of mind as insanity. Based upon the report from Henry and the letter from Neelly, maybe Jefferson decided that Meriwether Lewis was insane and took his own life."

"Except for one thing," said Mike.

"That's right," said Hollister, "the chalice and the gems. If Lewis wasn't telling the truth, where'd they come from?"

Mike was looking at photos of the chalice the forensic team had taken.

"We have any idea what these markings are? Generally, they look to be Native American . . . Central American maybe? So we're talking Mayans?"

"Or Aztec," said Hollister. "Look, I have taken the liberty of calling someone in to take a look at it. Hope you guys don't mind."

"Who would that be?" asked Jake.

"A young lady we worked with before. We confiscated a bunch of loot from a criminal ring we uncovered that was stealing and selling Native American artifacts. Once we confiscated all the stuff, we didn't know who it belonged to or where it should go, so we had to call someone in, and this young lady really did a job for us. She's good."

"Sounds like a plan to me," said Mike.

"I'm glad you think so," said a voice from behind them, as Charlotte Kosior entered the room.

She was a young lady in her late twenties, around 5'2" tall, slim, with green eyes, and long sandy hair.

All three men stood up as she approached and held out her hand, first to Jake.

"Mr. Sullivan, I've heard a lot about you. A pleasure."

Jake pointed to Hollister.

"We've just been hearing some nice things about you."

"Yeah, Jim over there is my buddy," she said, pointing to Hollister and smiling. "Mr. Lang, also a pleasure."

"No," said Mike, smiling back, "the pleasure is mine."

There was just the faintest trace of a blush on Miss Kosior's face, as Jake pulled up a chair for her and she sat down.

"So what do I need to look at, Jim?" she asked.

"Here," said Mike, handing her the photographs. "We're trying to determine exactly where this chalice came from."

She looked at the photographs Mike gave her and it didn't take her long.

"I'm pretty sure it's Aztec," she said. "Any chance I can see the real thing?"

"Sure," said Hollister. "C'mon, we'll go into the lab."

She again examined the actual chalice as it sat under glass, walking all around the case in which it was contained and noticing the gems that lay on a velvet cloth beside it.

"This is quite a find, boys," she said.

"Can you tell us what it means?" asked Mike.

"It tells a story of the Aztecs traveling down a great river by canoe, crossing an open sea, and coming to a land of much sun and warmth. I knew I was right!" she exclaimed.

"That you were right?" asked Jake.

"Most historians and experts in Native American cultures believe that the Aztecs migrated south from an area around the Four Corners."

"Four Corners?" asked Mike.

"The Four Corners is where Colorado, Utah, Arizona, and New Mexico all meet. From that area, they believe there was a land migration of what became the Aztec tribes through the southwestern United States, Mexico, and into Central America, to the Valley of Mexico, where the Aztec Empire bloomed. Part of this was based on artifacts that were found in the area and south of there, moving down to Central America, but I've examined those artifacts and I've always felt they were from a later era Aztec Empire, towards the end, really."

"So what's the river and the canoes telling you?" asked Jake.

"I think the Aztec tribe formulated farther north . . . that it formulated somewhere along the Missouri River and they followed the Missouri to the Mississippi and to the Gulf of Mexico. We found cuneiforms and other artifacts among North American Indian tribes that are translated into a story of dealing with great warriors from the south who traveled across the seas and of wars fought with these people."

"What about the artifacts you talked about?" asked Jake.

"Well, there is a legend that before Cortes destroyed the Aztec capitol of Tenochtitlan in 1521, Montezuma II sent most of the Aztec treasure north. I think the artifacts that have been found are part of the treasure that was taken north . . . not older artifacts from when the tribe migrated south. Although, I have to admit that something's always bothered me . . ."

"What's that?" said Mike.

"Well, if you are carrying treasure, what would lead you to lose pieces of it? I mean, these are items like the gold chalice that you have here. You'd know if they were lost. Why not retrieve them and take them with you?"

"Maybe Cortes's army was chasing them," said Mike.

"There's no historical record of that, and the Spanish were big-time record keepers. I must admit, though, I have had a thought."

"And?" said Jake.

"What if Montezuma II sent a party with a small amount of treasure north by land and the real purpose was to create a trail for the Spanish to follow if they decided to go after the treasure . . . and then sent the main body of the treasure to the Aztec home of origin, by the route they really knew? Load the treasure on canoes, go as they always did . . . across the Gulf . . . I don't know, I don't have any historical proof for it . . . it just makes more sense to me.. Did you ever feel anything in your gut?"

Mike started laughing.

"What do you find so funny?"

Mike pointed at Jake.

"Trust me, this is the king of gut instinct."

"I've read a lot about you," said Charlotte to Jake. "Your gut hasn't proven you wrong too many times."

"It just might be that yours hasn't either," he replied.

CHAPTER 18

Jake and Mike went through the whole thing, telling Charlotte all the details about Meriwether Lewis, his alleged discovery, the letters to Jefferson, Burwell Colbert's diary, and their finding of the chalice and the documents. She listened closely, making notes as she did so and asking questions when needing clarification. She then read through the documents again and again, studying the pictures of the chalice and the chalice, itself, scribbling down notes the entire time. She then studied her notepad, flipping through it again and again, and then finally setting it down in front of her and looked at Jake and Mike.

"Wow!" she said. "This is the coolest thing I've ever been involved in."

Jake and Mike looked at each other.

"No," she said, "this is the real deal. We're talking about the Legend of Montezuma's Treasure"

"The what?" asked Mike.

"C'mon, you guys have heard of this . . . haven't you?"

"Not really," said Jake.

"It's like I told you. Montezuma II allegedly sent his treasure north to keep it away from Cortes and the Spanish, who had invaded his country. A lot of people think it's somewhere in Kanab, Utah. There's a pond there, Three Lakes Pond, and these folks think the Aztecs hid their treasure in a cavern on the west side of the pond, sealed off the tunnel to it, and then diverted water to the pond they had created, to conceal it. But this . . . if my theory is right . . . makes more sense. Montezuma would have sent it back to the place of the tribe's beginning for safekeeping. I can't believe it. I can't believe I'm involved in this."

"Whoa," said Jake. "Just what do you think your involvement is?"

"What do you think?" she asked. "We've got to go to Montana."

"We?" asked Mike.

"You guys are going to need me. If we find anything, I'm the one that can identify it. C'mon . . . there's one more thing I've got to do and then let's go! I think there's a little airport in Three Forks."

"Slow down," said Jake. "We're under certain constraints here, which, unfortunately, I can't discuss with you. But we have to talk this over with some other folks and see how we're going to proceed."

"*If* we're going to proceed," said Mike.

"You can't let this go . . . this could be the discovery of a lifetime! Besides," she said, looking at Mike, that slight blush coming back to her cheeks, "what girl could resist going on a treasure hunt with the great Jake Sullivan and Mike Lang?"

And then it was Mike's turn to blush.

CHAPTER 19

After their meeting with Charlotte Kosior, Jake placed a call to Jason Bates and once again they were on the road to Washington . . . only this time to meet with President Fletcher.

Charlotte was going to stay at Quantico and keep reviewing the documents and the artifacts to see if she could come up with anything else, and she also wanted to place a call to a friend of hers, a Professor Peter Angelo at the University of Pittsburgh, which just happened to be Jake's alma mater. She explained that Angelo was an expert in the expedition of Lewis and Clark, which had actually started in Pittsburgh, and was very familiar with their journal and its entries, and she wanted to see if there were any entries dealing with the Three Forks area that could shed some light on what they were looking for.

"It's not just what she knows," said Jake, "she seems pretty insightful to me. Goes through information pretty quickly and comes to some pretty good conclusions."

"Well, we'll have to see. I mean, we haven't proven anything yet," said Mike.

"Sort of cute, too, don't you think?" asked Jake.

Mike started to shake his head.

"No, no . . . no you don't. Don't go there. No matchmaking. She's a professional. I'm a professional. We're doing a job. That's all."

"C'mon, Mike," said Jake. "I saw the way you two looked at each other."

"You know, you always say that. There was nothing about the way that we looked at each other. She's a very nice young lady . . . seems to be good at her job."

"You know, you're right," said Jake. "Really, if you think about it, she's done what we need her to do. There's no sense in her going with us if we get the okay to head out to Montana."

There was silence from Mike, and then . . . .

"Well, I've been thinking about that. She might be of some use to us, Jake. We don't know what we're going to find. I mean, we're going to be in an area where there have been a lot of Indian tribes. We're going to have to have someone be able to identify the artifacts and see where they came from if we find anything."

"Yeah, but we can do that after the fact."

"It might be better if we have someone on site to help us out."

"Nothing between you two, huh?"

"It's a professional conclusion I came to, all right? That's all. Nothing more."

"Whatever you say, Mike . . . whatever you say."

THE WHITE HOUSE
WASHINGTON, D.C.

CHAPTER 20

Jason Bates ushered Jake and Mike into the Oval Office, and President Jordan Fletcher arose from behind his desk and came out to shake their hands.

"Jake . . . Mike . . . good to see you."

"A pleasure, Mr. President," they both said.

"So what's this I hear about another treasure hunt involving you two?"

"We're not quite sure yet," said Jake, "but it looks like there could be something there, and given the fact that Adam Colbert was tortured and killed after he came to see me, it appears that there might be someone else interested."

"As I understand from Jason, you think that someone might be Group 45?"

"Their finances have taken a hit, Mr. President," said Mike. "Remember what ISIS did down in Jamaica."

"I remember very well, Mr. Lang," said the President. "I have to be honest . . . my chief concern right now is the chatter we've heard about a planned attack on this country."

"I've been thinking about that, too, " said Jake. "If this operation is real, it's taken a lot of time, a lot of manpower, and a lot of expense . . . and if Group 45 is involved, maybe they're looking for resources to make a final payment."

Fletcher went back around his desk and sat down.

"I certainly wouldn't put anything past them, but don't you think the connection is a little tenuous?"

"There was something that Joan Taylor said to me in Mexico, Mr. President. She said she always had eyes on me. If she was telling the truth, they'd have known about Colbert. If they discovered his diary, they'd know about the chalice and gems, and if they have as much reach as we think they do into our own government, they could easily know about what we found at Poplar Forest."

Just then, Bates's phone buzzed.

"I'm sorry. . . excuse me . . . I have to take this, Mr. President. It might be about Miami."

"Go ahead, Jason," and Bates hurried from the room.

"It's a point worth considering, Jake."

"My problem is I'd rather have you in Miami right now than Montana."

"Mr. President, I don't mean to interrupt you, but given computers and phones and the other means and methods that are available to us today, we can stay on top of Miami even though we're in Montana," said Mike.

"I understand, but I'm an old Marine. There's nothing like boots on the ground . . . but . . . I trust you two. You haven't let me down yet, and I tend to think that if it's your belief that it's more than likely that there's something there, then that's my belief, too. So, I suppose what we should do . . .' and just then the door opened and Bates came into the room.

"I apologize, Mr. President, I didn't mean to interrupt."

There was a look of concern on Bates's face that the President instantly recognized.

"What is it, Jason? What's wrong?"

Jake looked at Mike.

"Jake . . . I'm sorry. The young lady that's been working with you . . . Charlotte Kosior . . . she was assaulted last night on her way home."

Mike jumped up.

"Is she all right?!"

"Roughed up a little bit, but yes . . . but whatever she was carrying was taken from her."

"A notepad," said Jake, looking at Mike.

"What notepad?" asked the President.

"Notes about the whole thing, Mr. President . . . everything we found out so far and where we think it leads."

Fletcher slammed his fist on the desk.

"And now the enemy has it! That settles it! Get yourselves to Montana. If there's anything there, Group 45 or anyone else can get their hands on it."

"Understood, Mr. President," said Jake.

"We'll move on it right away," said Mike. "Where is she?" he said to Bates.

"They brought her back to Quantico. She's in the Med Unit there."

"Right after we see Charlotte Kosior," said Mike, turning to the President.

"I understand, Mr. Lang, and I agree. Now, be on your way." Looking at Bates, Fletcher then said, "Stay here, Jason. We have things to discuss," and Jake and Mike headed out the door.

MED UNIT
QUANTICO, VIRGINIA

CHAPTER 21

Charlotte Kosior had been sleeping, a bandage across her forehead, her lower lip cracked, and her right eye blackened. When she opened her eyes, everything was blurry at first, and then she saw Mike Lang seated by her bedside.

"Hey, how you feeling?" asked Mike.

"Like I got hit by a truck."

"Who was it?" said Mike, the anger evident in his voice.

"I don't know. There were two of them. They got me from behind. I wouldn't give them my bag, and that's when they decided to get a little rough. It could have been worse. One of my neighbors came out when he heard the ruckus and scared them away, but they got my bag."

"So, now they know everything we know."

"Why do you say that?" said Charlotte.

"The yellow legal pad," said Mike.

"I'm not stupid, Mr. Lang. That pad was sent to my office by special courier. You think I'd carry it around with me on the streets of Washington?"

Mike laughed to himself.

"Jake was right. You are smart."

"Well I'm glad one of you thinks so."

"My apologies," said Mike. "And please . . . call me Mike and not Mr. Lang."

She smiled at him.

"I guess your apology is accepted . . . Mike. And you can call me Charlie . . . that's what everybody in my family calls me."

"You know, I've been meaning to ask you something . . . your last name . . . you don't have any relatives doing any type of work for the Israelis, do you?"

"No, why do you ask?" she said.

"Oh, I just know somebody who uses that last name every once in a while."

"Sorry, I don't. Maybe if you tell me a little bit more, I can find out for you."

"Sorry, that's all I'm at liberty to say."

"You guys are real cloak and dagger," she said, smiling. "I like it. Now, what happened with the President?"

"We're on our way to Montana."

"Good. Let's get me out of here and get going."

"Whoa, whoa, whoa . . . take it easy. You need to recover from this."

"I'll recover much better on a treasure hunt than I will sitting in this hospital. Nurse!" she cried out, as Mike just smiled and shook his head.

MIAMI, FLORIDA

CHAPTER 22

Charlotte Kosior, at her insistence, was released from the hospital and was booked on a government jet to Three Forks Airport.

Jake and Mike also took a government jet, but to their offices in Miami, as the President insisted, to make sure that all operations relative to the Port of Miami were operational and to their satisfaction. While there, they received an email from Charlotte passing on the information she had received from Peter Angelo at the University of Pittsburgh, who had sent her the excerpts from the journal of Lewis and Clark relative to their time in the Three Forks area.

"Listen to this," Mike said to Jake as he read the email. "That professor at your old school sent some information to Charlie. Clark set out to look for Shoshone Indians, leaving Lewis alone to explore the area near Three Forks, but had to return because he developed a fever. That's the way Lewis was described at the time he died . . . seemingly disoriented and having a high fever. Okay, here are Lewis's descriptions," said Mike, "and what he found."

"Between the middle and southeast Forks, near their junction with the southwest Fork, there is a handsome site for a fortification. It consists of a limestone rock of oblong form. Its size perpendicular and about twenty-five feet high, except at the extremity

toward the middle Fork, where it ascends gradually and like the top, is covered with a fine turf or greensward. The top is level and contains about two acres. The rock rises from the level plain as if it had been designed for some such purpose."

"It seems he attached some significance to it," said Jake.

"Enough to go back a couple years later and do some exploring. He was the governor of the territory. He could have left St. Louis at any time and headed west . . . supposedly to work out agreements with the Indian tribes, dealings with the fur trappers . . . anything."

"Anything else?" asked Jake.

"No, that was it. She just said she'll see us in Montana. Wonder what this means . . ."

"What?" asked Jake.

"Well, her email block says 'Charlotte Rose Kosior' and then beneath it 'FINS'. What the hell is 'FINS'?"

"Look it up in the directory."

"Okay, okay . . . I just thought you might know. You seem to know everything else."

"Don't get testy, Mike. You'll be with her soon."

"Again with this?" said Mike as he picked up the Federal Directory of Agencies. Ahh . . . here we are . . . 'FINS' . . . Federal Institute of Native Studies. She's the Director!"

"Wow. Born and raised in Santa Clara, studied Native American Studies at Stanford, got her Ph.D. there, too."

"Makes sense. Like I told you before," said Jake, "she knows what she's doing . . . at least professionally. I'm not sure about her personal evaluations."

And with that, Mike threw the Registry across the room as Jake laughed and ducked and moved out of the way.

THREE FORKS, MONTANA

CHAPTER 23

Early the next morning, all final decisions about the situation regarding the Port of Miami having been made, Jake and Mike boarded a government jet and headed to the Three Forks Airport. Eva had made reservations for all of them at the Sacajawea Lodge in Three Forks, Montana, and Bates had provided Jake with a file giving the details of how things would play out, should they discover anything.

Charlotte met them at the airport with a rented SUV and drove them to the lodge, where they had dinner and discussed their plans for the next day.

When dinner was over, Jake excused himself to go to his room and call Linda and his girls to see how things were on the home front.

Mike and Charlotte drifted out onto the patio.

"This is such beautiful country," said Charlotte, as the sun started to set. "It's just amazing being here." As she turned to speak to Mike, she brushed against him and took a step back.

"I agree. Everything here is beautiful," he said, looking directly at her. "Can't think of a place I'd rather be."

Again, she blushed and smiled.

"C'mon," he said, "I'll walk you to your room."

When they arrived at her door, she used her card to unlock it and turned to Mike.

"Thank you for the escort, sir," she said. "I'll see you in the morning."

"Indeed you will," he said, "and you're quite welcome."

She closed the door behind her and leaned with her back against it and thought to herself, *"Indeed I will, Mr. Lang, indeed I will."*

CHAPTER 24

The next morning, the three of them traveled out to the Three Forks of the Missouri. Charlotte looked at a photo she had copied from a website dealing with Lewis and Clark and their time in Montana and pointed to a tall, cylindrical limestone formation to their left.

"That's 'Lewis's Rock.' The description that Professor Angelo gave me from Lewis's journal described what he saw from the top of that. I think we should climb it and take a look."

They got their equipment out of the back of the SUV and made their way to the base of the stone formation. Climbing up from one of the sides was not difficult given the sloping nature of the terrain, and they reached the summit without incident. The view was breathtaking.

The Gallatin River flowed before them and across it was a huge limestone formation, 'Fort Rock,' as it was called. The Jefferson River was beyond it, part of it hidden from view by the mesa itself, while the Missouri flowed from where the Jefferson and Madison met, beginning its long trek to the Mississippi.

"So," said Mike, "this treasure we're looking for is supposed to be inside that flat rock across the river from us?"

"That's the idea," said Jake.

Mike looked at Charlie, who had not answered, and she stared, as if in a trance, at the view before her. She was seeing it as it existed hundreds of years before, when the rivers flowed out of a small inland sea, in the center of which sat a rock formation . . . a rock formation that had been created into a temple. Woven canoes were on the waterways before her, and as time passed and the lake drained, the inhabitants moved on, down the Missouri to the Mississippi and beyond, to a new city in a lake.

"Charlie?" said Mike. "Charlie."

She came out of her reverie and looked from Mike to Jake and back again.

"It's here. This was the birthplace of the Aztec civilization, and that rock was the base of their first temple, and inside it was their first and last treasury."

Jake looked at Mike.

"I won't argue with her. We just have to find our way inside."

"C'mon," said Charlie, "let's go. We have to get over there."

"Charlie?" asked Jake in a low voice, smiling.

"It's her family nickname. It's what she likes to be called. She told me."

"That's the point, isn't it, Mike? She told you," and he moved on ahead of him, leaving Mike standing there, his hands held out in an act of frustration as Jake and Charlie headed down the trail in front of him.

CHAPTER 25

The Gallatin was low and they were able to wade across it without difficulty and walked around the base of the mesa, Charlotte carefully looking at it as she did. They made a complete circle and ended up at the sloping base where they had started, which would allow them to climb to the top.

"Well, that walk sort of proves what Andrew Henry wrote in his letter to Jefferson. He couldn't find an entrance to this thing. I didn't see anything looking up the slopes or at the base that showed a way in," said Jake.

"I didn't either," said Mike.

"Well, it's here," said Charlie, "we just have to find it."

"Let's head up to the top," said Jake. "Maybe the view will inspire us."

It was a beautiful day and the tourists were out in droves, walking all over the area. In their hiking gear, Jake, Mike, and Charlie looked like the rest of them, not in any way out of place, as they moved about the surface and took photographs. They paid no attention to another man and woman dressed in similar fashion, except for the small earpieces they each had, and the fact that one of them, at all times, was keeping Jake, Mike, and Charlie within view.

The three spent the better part of the day examining the surface of the rock, again going down to the base, and moving down the sides where they could. As sun set, they went back up to the top, hoping the view would soothe the sting of their failure in finding any entrance to the former temple of the Aztecs.

"Damn!" said Charlie. "I just can't believe it. I know it's here."

Jake walked to the edge and looked out over the Jefferson River, taking in the spectacular view that reached out for miles before him, and then he looked down at the river, and then he went back to Mike and Charlie.

"Charlie, your theory, if I understand it, is that Montezuma sent his treasure up the Mississippi and then the Missouri to this site by canoe, am I right?"

"That's my theory," she said.

"And you both would agree that we've been all over this rock and we can't find a way into it, right?" and they both nodded. "And we think the treasure is in a cavern somewhere inside . . . which would mean that there *has* to be an opening by which the treasure from the canoes got inside."

"This sounds like my old logic professor," said Mike. "What are you getting at, Jake?"

Jake looked at Charlie.

"If the treasure got inside and there's no opening on the rock, there has to be an opening somewhere else. And if you were unloading treasure from a canoe, what would be the easiest way to do it?"

Charlie punched Jake in the arm.

"To unload it in the water."

"Exactly," he said. "Follow me," and he took them to the edge. "Now, obviously these rivers would have looked different several hundred years ago, and now there are more silt deposits. If you remember Meriwether Lewis's letter to Jefferson, he said, '*I looked at the rivers that lay below me and I imagined them as they had looked hundreds of years before, and then the answer came to me.'* Look beyond the silt . . . right down there."

"I don't see anything," said Mike.

"I do," said Charlie. "The shade of the water changes. It's lighter out in the water, and it's darker the closer it gets to shore, and it should be the opposite. It should be deeper in the middle and more shallow as it approaches."

"My guess is there is access to a tunnel. Probably covered by hundreds of years' worth of silt and other runoff, but . . . it's worth a shot, right?"

Charlie started pacing back and forth, deep in thought.

"It couldn't be a water trap like in Utah. They used this as a temple because the lake was already here."

"Do you know what she's talking about?" whispered Jake.

"Just let her work it out," said Mike.

Charlie went on, "But with the seasonal rise and fall of the rivers, there could have been a period when the cavern entrance was accessible . . . a time for ritual and celebration . . . a time for a ceremonial chalice."

She turned and pointed at Jake.

"Everything I've read about you is true, Jake. We need to get equipment and get down there and get a closer look at this. The treasure is here! Let's head back to the hotel," and she started down the slope.

"So, what do you think, Mike?"

"It appears you might have done it again, Jake."

"You don't seem too enthused."

"No, no . . . it's fine," said Mike. "Everything's good. Good thinking."

Jake walked over to Mike and put his hand on his shoulder.

"Don't worry, buddy. Everything is okay. She's probably read good things about you, too," and he slapped him on the arm and then turned and headed down the slope.

"You know . . . there are times . . ." said Mike, as he muttered to himself, following after Jake.

The only other couple on the mesa soon followed their departure.

CHAPTER 26

Back at the hotel, Jake called Jason Bates and explained to him what they had found and made arrangements for a dive team from the closest military installation.

They had just finished dinner when his encrypted phone rang.

"Mr. Sullivan, this is Colonel Jackson Tillman from Malmstrom Air Force Base in Great Falls, about one hundred fifty miles north of your location. I understand you need a dive team. Tell me a little bit about the where and when."

Without going into details, Jake explained that they believed there was an entrance to a cavern that began on a river bottom in the Three Forks area.

"Three Forks, huh? Well, most of the trains on the track near that area have a light schedule at night, and there isn't much tourist traffic in the dark, so I think two men at nighttime would be our best shot. Anything else you need to tell me?"

"We might be under surveillance by the bad guys."

"Understood. This phone is encrypted?"

"It is," said Jake.

"We will formulate a plan and be in touch tomorrow, with a tentative go for tomorrow night at midnight."

"I'll await your call, Colonel."

They moved to the patio for a final cup of coffee, where Jake told them of his conversation with Colonel Tillman.

"Well, boys," said Charlie, "we're getting closer."

"If we're right," said Mike.

"Jake's conclusion makes sense to me," said Charlie, sipping at her coffee.

By this point, Jake had also taken to calling Charlotte "Charlie".

"You, see? Charlie agrees with my conclusion."

"Oh, I understand," said Mike. "I'm not saying you aren't. You're usually right . . . just not all the time."

"Well," said Jake, getting up, "I'm going to turn in. I have some calls to make first. I'll check on Miami and let you know what I find out."

"Sounds good," said Mike.

"Oh!" said Jake as he turned to look back at Mike. "Thanks for that vote of confidence, by the way. I appreciate it," and he headed out.

"I think you hurt his feelings," said Charlie.

"Nah, we're always like that."

"Something bothering you, Mike?"

"No, no, no . . . everything's fine."

"Okay," said Charlie. "I was just checking. Think I'm going to turn in, too."

"Okay . . . well, let me walk you to your room."

They arrived at Charlie's door and she once again opened it with her key card. Then she turned to Mike and pulled him close and kissed him a long, lingering kiss, and she looked into his eyes and whispered to him, "You don't have to be jealous of Jake. You're the one that's here," and she pulled him into her room and closed the door behind them.

CHAPTER 27

The next morning Jake found Mike at the restaurant reading the morning paper. He put it down and looked at Jake.

"How's everything in Miami?"

"Nothing new so far. Everything seems to be a go. Hey, remember that investigation you were doing on that cartel out of Paraguay?"

"Yeah. Sure I do," said Mike.

"Eva left me a message about it. Who'd you hand that off to?"

"Trafford," said Mike.

"All right. I've got to get in touch with him."

"Problems?"

"No, not really. Just got some new information and I want to give him the name of the contact."

"I can do it if you want me to."

"Yeah, that sounds good. Probably be best coming from you anyway. I think I'm going to get some breakfast," said Jake, as he looked around for a waitress.

"You know, Jake," said Mike, "I didn't mean anything last night."

"What are you talking about?" asked Jake.

"I didn't want you to get the wrong idea that I was trying to make you look bad or anything."

"Thought never entered into my mind, Mike. What made you ask?"

"Nothing . . . well, just after what Charlie said."

"What was that?"

"She doesn't understand how we talk to each other. She was concerned that maybe . . . you know . . . I hurt your feelings or something."

"Did you explain to her that that's the way we are and everything's okay?"

"I did, yeah."

"And she understands?"

"I think so."

"You know, I think I'm going to skip breakfast and go for a walk. It's a beautiful morning."

"All right. Well, we'll meet up this afternoon and go over our plans for tonight then. What time is he supposed to call you?"

"He didn't say. He just said he'd call. Don't forget to call Trafford."

"No, no . . . I'll take care of it," said Mike.

"And you're sure Charlie's okay with everything?"

"Yeah, like I said, I talked to her and everything seems okay."

"You had enough time?"

"Yeah, sure. Why?"

"Well, I figured you had enough time . . . 'cause I called you about three o'clock in the morning when I found out about this information I had to get to the guy you handed the investigation off to and no one answered in your room."

Mike looked up at him and just shook his head.

"Well played."

"I thought so," said Jake, smiling. "I'll talk to you later," and with that, he headed out the door.

CHAPTER 28

Colonel Tillman did call at about two o'clock in the afternoon and explained to Jake how the mission was going to work.

"There are going to be three folks dressed like you, who somewhat resemble you three, take your car and head out of town. There will be another car left in its place with the keys under the mat. It'll have a Montana plate, number A63 H25. We'll have a tail on the vehicle that drives away to make sure whoever's been watching you follows it out of town. It's not going to come back until tomorrow, and when it does, we'll again move it from the hotel and you can use the new vehicle we're providing you. Hopefully, there is only one set of eyes on you and they won't be around to watch us tonight. We've had a man out there posing as a geologist, taking silt samples along the river. He thinks he's made out a stone formation that could be steps, so we have a pin-pointed location for tonight. Myself and one of my men will hike in from a couple miles out with our gear, and we'll meet you right where you think the steps should be. If we're not there, walk around the base until you find us . . . your location might be off. It's supposed to be clear tonight with a good moon, so hopefully, you won't need flashlights or anything else. We've left night vision goggles in the vehicle for all three of you. If you have any trouble, put those on and that should help you out. If we find a tunnel, we'll follow it. If it leads to a cavern, we'll go in it, and we'll photograph whatever is there. Mr. Sullivan, we understand this is a military op and a top secret one, at that. That's the classification we've been given from the highest authority, so you can be assured that other than my man, who I have hand-picked, and myself, no one else is going to know what we find, other than the three of you."

"It seems to be a sound plan, Colonel, and I appreciate your assurances."

"Understood," said the Colonel. "We'll see you out there at 24:00 hours," and he signed off.

Jake found Charlie and Mike sitting on the patio and motioned for them to come meet with him at the railing, where he whispered to them the information he received from Colonel Tillman.

"So, tonight we find out," said Mike.

"It'll be there. I know it will," said Charlie.

"Don't set yourself up for disappointment, Charlie . . . so far it's all guesswork."

"No it isn't. I'm just like you, Jake . . . I feel it in my gut."

CHAPTER 29

Jake, Mike, and Charlie went out to the parking lot at 11:30 and quickly found the SUV that had been left for them. They drove out to the parking area, got out, took the night goggles with them, and using them and the moonlight, made their way along the base of the mesa to the spot where Jake thought the steps would be located. There was no sign of Tillman where Jake thought he would be, but it turned out he was only about twenty-five yards off when they encountered Tillman and a Lieutenant Sutton.

Whispered introductions were made and Tillman made sure their equipment was operating properly and gave the signal for he and Sutton to head into the river.

Jake, Mike, and Charlie watched as they went below the surface and sat down on some rocks to wait. Every minute seemed like an eternity.

"It's a good sign that they're not coming out," said Charlie.

"Unless they ran into the base of the mesa and are moving along under water to see if they can find an opening that isn't there," said Jake.

"C'mon, you two. Stick with your gut. If you think it's here, it's here," said Mike.

It was actually forty-seven minutes on the nose when Tillman and Sutton broke the surface of the water and made their way to them.

"Well?" said Jake.

"Mission accomplished, Mr. Sullivan."

He handed him a waterproof pouch, containing a camera.

"Here's your photos. You found yourself one hell of a treasure."

"Yes!" exclaimed Charlie, as quietly as possible, as she dug her nails into Mike's arm.

They formed a circle. Tillman pulled out a penlight and ran the photos through the camera's viewer.

"There were two caverns . . . one primarily holding works of hammered gold and silver, and a smaller cavern full of leather pouches, each one full of precious gems . . . rubies, emeralds, jade . . . some cut in forms or figures and others still in pure mineral form.

This was well engineered. A wide tunnel and upward shaft with hand holds cut in. It appears the floor of the cavern was chiseled into a bowl shape . . . probably to contain water as the rivers and lake rose. The treasure was packed onto ledges cut into the walls and other high points in the caverns – by the feel of the leather containers, there was very little water damage over the years.

The tunnel and shaft up were relatively short . . . we could have made it without gear. And as you can see . . . someone did," as he came to a close up of the cavern wall where "M Lewis 8 August 1809" was carved. "There were also skeletons of approximately a dozen men, each one with a spear stuck in the approximate place where the heart would be, one lying on top of another. We could picture them all committing suicide by stabbing each other, except for the last, who would ensure that they were all dead and then take his own life. He was lying farther apart from the rest, and he had been the last one alive. It's an amazing sight in there."

"Now that we've made the discovery," said Jake, "is the rest of the plan going to occur as it was outlined to me by Bates?"

"It should be on the news about noon tomorrow. Everything will start moving after that. I'd say to come out here about two o'clock in the afternoon and everything should be ready for you."

"Thank you, gentlemen. Hell of a job."

"Thank you . . . hell of a find," said Tillman. "Let's go, Sutton. We've got a long hike."

"All right, you two," said Jake. "Let's head back to the car and I'll tell you the plan as Bates described it to me."

Charlie couldn't control herself. She hugged Jake.

"We did it! We actually found it! We did it!" and then she hugged Mike and kissed him.

They couldn't see him in the dark as he headed back to the SUV, but Jake was smiling, happy for his best friend and a fine young lady.

CHAPTER 30

The elation of their discovery wore off to some degree as they arrived back at the lodge and Jake informed them of the details involving recovery of the treasure.

Once again, they found themselves alone on the patio with a brisk wind coming in from the northwest.

"There's going to be a fake train derailment on the tracks adjacent to the site," Jake began, "and allegedly a toxic substance entered the Jefferson River as a result. This will give them the means to call in a hazmat team, which will really be a Delta Force team with engineering units from Malmstrom to seal off the area and do a cleanup of the river. As I understand it, they'll bring in a huge backhoe on a flatbed on the train tracks to dredge the river bottom. Prior to this, a team will be sent in to the tunnel and then the shaft up into the caverns. The folks will have special containers, which they will fill with the artifacts and gems, and when the backhoe goes into the water to dredge the bottom, another team of divers will place containers in the bucket with the silt so when the bucket is emptied into the trucks, the treasure container will actually go in with the debris and silt that has been extracted."

"How long do they think the operation will take?" asked Mike.

"They don't know yet. Depends how may containers it's going to take to empty the caverns, but things are going to move fast . . . I know that. You heard Tillman. There's supposed to be a news story at noon tomorrow about a train derailment. What I got from my conversation with Bates was that this plan was in place and ready to go."

"And we're supposed to be out there about two o'clock?" asked Mike.

"That's what the man said."

"I have a question," said Charlotte. "What happens to the cavern? Those photographs we looked at showed detailed writings on the cavern walls. That place is a historical treasure, as well as a site of financial treasure. What happens to it?"

"I thought that might be a concern," said Jake, "so I made it clear to Bates that there had to be some consideration given to that aspect of this operation, and he assured me that the plan was to remove any and all findings, now including the artifacts, gems, and the skeletons of the warriors, and take them to a holding area/laboratory that is already being prepared at Malmstrom.

As for the caverns themselves, they will not be touched, other than for the removal of the items in question, and at some later date, a discovery will be announced, and the process will begin as it always does with the discovery of any historical find."

"I hope everybody knows what they're doing," said Charlie, sitting back in her chair.

"I think we'll be all right," said Jake. "They're using a forensic team led by your friend, Jim Hollister. I'm pretty sure he'll understand the significance of what he's dealing with."

"I think you're right," said Mike. "Seemed like a good guy, and he seemed to know what he was doing."

"Then I guess all I can hope for," said Charlie, "is that they have a good supervisor on hand in the lab at Malmstrom to make sure everything is properly taken care of."

"I don't think that's going to be a worry either," said Jake.

"And just why is that?" asked Charlie.

"Because the supervisor is going to be you."

"What? Me?" asked Charlie.

"I explained to Bates that I couldn't think of a better person and he readily agreed."

Charlie was in shock.

"I . . . I don't know what to say, Jake. Thank you!"

"Not a problem. You deserve it."

"Nice work, Jake," said Mike, smiling and tipping his bottle of Rainier toward him. "And," he said, looking at Charlie, "he's right. You do deserve it."

"Well," said Jake, standing up and stretching, "I'm going to try and get some rest. Looks like it's only a few hours before daybreak. We have to get our gear together and be out at the site by two, so I'll see you in the morning."

After Jake left, Mike got up and put his hand down to Charlie, who was still seated.

"Want me to walk you back?"

"No, thanks Mike. I think I'm just going to sit here for a while and let this all sink in."

"Then I'll say goodnight," said Mike, and he reached down and kissed her. "See you in a couple hours."

Charlie settled into her chair and took a sip from her own bottle of Rainier and waited for the approaching dawn and smiled, having never felt so good about the career she had chosen for herself. One of the most fantastic finds in history . . . working with Jake Sullivan . . . and what seemed to be developing with Mike . . . she'd never been happier. She pulled her jacket around her against the wind and waited for the dawn.

CHAPTER 31

It was almost noon when Mike and Charlie came into Jake's room. Their eyes were glued on a game show playing out on television when the news flash they were waiting for appeared. They listened as a reporter gave the initial story.

> "We have just learned that a Montana Rail Link
> Special has derailed near Three Forks. Evidently,
> some of the cars contained toxic materials from drilling
> sites to the north. Given the concern of a potentially
> hazardous condition, it has been closed off to the
> general public and is being evacuated. Federal
> hazmat teams are being sent in and a no-fly zone
> has been established over the entire area. We have
> no further details as to the cause of the derailment,
> nor as to the substances that may have entered the
> Jefferson River at the derailment site. A hiker in
> the area captured the incident on video, and we
> play that for you now."

The three watched as the video rolled and showed a car leaving the tracks and sliding down the embankment, becoming partially submerged in the Jefferson River, and then the video abruptly ended.

> "It is our further understanding that federal resources

*are being gathered and equipment is already on its way
to the site to deal with this situation. We will keep
you updated as more information becomes available
throughout the day, at what might possibly be a
serious insult to one of the most scenic areas of
Montana."*

With that, Jake dropped the remote and silenced the reporter.

"Typical," said Mike, shaking his head. "They have no idea what it is, but already it's a disaster."

"Actually, that's sort of what we were hoping for, isn't it?" asked Jake.

"I know," said Mike, "but these guys really tick me off sometimes."

Jake looked at his watch.

"We have an hour. Everybody get their gear together. We'll meet out at the Jeep."

Mike and Charlie got up and headed out the door. Once outside, Mike stopped her.

"Well, did you make it to dawn?"

"No," she laughed. "I dozed off and went back to my room and tried to get a couple hours of sleep, but it didn't really work. I guess I just should have stayed there."

"Everything okay?"

"Everything is fine," she said. "I'll see you down at the Jeep," and she kissed him on the cheek and headed to her room.

CHAPTER 32

Once the Jeep was loaded, Jake pulled out with Mike in the front passenger seat and Charlie in the rear, and headed out to the site.

They were amazed when they got there to see what had happened in so short a period of time. A whole camp had sprung up. There was machinery and equipment and Quonset huts set up as temporary quarters for the workers to stay in.

There was also a perimeter around the site with vehicles, saw horses, and guards to keep out reporters and sight-seers, and, of course, as the three of them knew, anyone else who might be interested in the discovery.

There was a three-word password that had been given to them by Commander Tillman that was going to be changed at 8:00 A.M. and 8:00 P.M. each day the operation was ongoing, and as Jake approached the guard, he said, "Halls of Montezuma." The guard allowed them to enter and directed them to a Quonset hut close to his post, explaining that they could pick up ID badges there and be assigned their quarters.

As Jake entered the hut, the men and women who were there, who were otherwise occupied with paperwork and moving back and forth from desk to desk, stopped what they were doing and came to attention.

"Thank you, but there's no need. Please, go about your business," said Jake.

"What's all this about," asked Mike.

"Bates determined that I should be in charge of the operation, on orders from the President. Obviously, the word has been given to everybody."

Mike and Charlie looked at each other and Charlie smiled sheepishly and asked, "We don't have to call you boss or anything, do we?"

Jake looked at them both.

"No . . . sir will be sufficient," and turned and walked over to the desk where a young lady was holding up ID cards for the three of them.

They were assigned their quarters, with Jake and Mike occupying one and Charlie in another. The miniature Quonset huts were no more than glorified tents with metal rather than canvas sides, but they served a purpose.

After stowing their gear, they met outside and headed toward the operation center, where they introduced themselves to the "foreman", who was actually another Delta officer by the name of Thomas Heller. Heller held out his hand to each of them.

"Mr. Sullivan . . . Mr. Lang . . . Miss Kosior. Welcome to the operation"

"So," said Jake, "what's our time frame?"

It had been determined that there would be no reference to the treasure or to their status. Bates and Jake had concluded that it was a given that he would be followed to the site and that he would be under observation of some type. That is why the discovery attempt was done at night and, hopefully, so far as Group 45 or anyone else was concerned, the discovery had never happened. The derailment itself had been well-staged, with a driver inside the car that had been rigged with its own steering system. All the driver had to do was press a button and the car disconnected, and then he simply steered it off the tracks and down the slope to the river, and he wasn't extricated until the site had been sealed. The video, of course, had been made by a member of Delta Force, mostly with computer graphics.

It had been determined that all with knowledge of the actual reason for the dredging would act out an elaborate charade, as if a toxic spill had actually occurred.

In answer to Jake's question, Heller responded, "Well, Mr. Sullivan, the spill covered a lot more area than we thought. We've got it contained, but I think we're going to have to remove about twenty truckloads from the river bottom. Fortunately, the toxin that was being carried dissipates in water, but there is a heavier portion to it that settles at the bottom we are going to have to dredge. We're going to dig down ten feet since silt's pretty compacted. As long as we don't run into any problems, we should be out of here the day after tomorrow."

The rest of their conversation had been choreographed, as well.

"If I might ask, Mr. Sullivan, why are you out here? Why are you in charge of this?"

"I'm working with the federal prosecutor in Bozeman. There's been some cartel activity with some of the groups operating in my jurisdiction down in Miami and it appears they've established a distribution point in Montana. We're trying to see if we can form a joint task force to do something about it, so, since I was here when this happened, I was the ranking federal official in the area. Homeland Security, in all their wisdom, decided I should be here, and here I am."

Heller laughed.

"I know what you mean . . . federal bureaucracy . . . you just can't beat it."

"Amen to that," said Mike, and they continued with the briefing.

After it was completed, the three walked around the site. Jake and Mike had decided they wanted to familiarize themselves as much as possible with the faces of the men they were dealing with, so if they noticed a stranger among them, they could take the necessary action. As Tillman indicated, he was no longer on site, nor was Lieutenant Sutton. This group was engineers and forensic specialists, with only the perimeter guards being Delta Force.

But Jake had the feeling that Tillman was somewhere out there, lurking about. He had given Jake a number to enter into his encrypted phone where he could be reached twenty-four hours a day . . . a call that Jake hoped he would not have to make.

But others were also watching, and they had different plans.

CHAPTER 33

The second day on site passed without incident. The dredger worked continuously, clawing the river bottom for silt and depositing it and containers of discovered treasure into one specially fitted truck after another, which were moved into a guarded lot after loading, waiting for the operation to complete.

Heller met up with them in the mess tent, where they were having their evening meal.

"Worked out pretty much as I planned," he said. "We'll have the final trucks loaded tomorrow and the word is they move out at midnight for Malmstrom. They follow Route 287 for about 150 miles to the base, with an armored guard in the front and rear."

"Nice work, Mr. Heller," said Jake, extending his hand. "A job well done."

Heller laughed, "We're not there yet. Let's hope so. Now, if you'll excuse me, I have some things that need tended to," and then he looked at Charlie. "Ma'am, there is one other thing," and he moved toward her and sat down beside her, his back to the table. "If I may, ma'am," he said in a soft voice, "the powers that be would like you to leave tonight and head up to Malmstrom."

"Wait a minute," said Mike, "we don't know who or what is out there."

"Understood, Mr. Lang," said Heller, "but I can assure you, we're taking all precautions. Miss Kosior, are you ready?"

"I am," Charlie replied.

Part of the briefing that Jake had given them about his conversation with Bates and the plan that would go into effect included Charlie leaving the night before the final trucks were loaded to go to Malmstrom and make sure the lab had everything she needed to take care of what would be delivered.

"I still don't like this," said Mike.

Heller looked at him and spoke softly.

"Back roads the whole way. One of our drivers."

"I should go, too."

Jake shook his head in the negative.

"I don't like it," Mike said, staring at Jake. "I should go, too."

Heller continued to speak softly.

"Won't work. Husband and wife . . . tourists coming back from a day of sightseeing . . . heading back to their hotel in Great Falls . . . it's all set up."

Charlie moved over and sat by Mike.

"It's a good plan. I'll be fine."

She looked at Heller.

"When?"

"Fifteen minutes . . . right outside."

"I'll be ready," she said.

After Heller left, Charlie got up.

"Well, since I'm all packed, I think I'm going to have some dessert. Anybody care to join me?"

"I'm good," said Jake, but Mike wouldn't answer, so she headed toward the chow line.

"She's a good woman, Mike. She's smart and she's tough. She'll be okay."

Mike just shook his head.

"I've heard that too many times before, Jake," and he got up and walked outside.

Charlie came back and sat down with a piece of apple pie and began eating. Without looking up, she asked Jake, "Is he going to be all right?"

"It's hard for him. Things haven't worked out in the past and he cares for you."

"I know," she said, and then set down her fork. She sighed and grabbed her gear from underneath the bench where she was sitting and walked over to Jake and kissed him on the cheek. "I'll see you at Malmstrom, Mr. Sullivan."

"You can count on it, Miss Kosior."

Outside, she found Mike sitting on a bench, and she sat down beside him.

"I just wanted to tell you I'll see you tomorrow," she said.

He looked at her.

"Promise?"

"Promise."

"There's your ride," said Mike.

She smiled at him and kissed him and headed for the vehicle that pulled to a stop, and Mike watched it until it made the first bend and it was no longer in his line of sight.

CHAPTER 34

Jake rose early and made his way to the top of the mesa.

There was now a deep blue pool of water near the tunnel entrance, approximately fifty feet in circumference, where shallows of silt had been before. He turned and looked in all directions, the sun rising on the wildflowers, spreading off in a vast field beyond the river, the field broken only here and there by large formations of limestone; otherwise, flowing as far as the eye could see. The mountain range was silhouetted against the sky far in the distance. He thought about Mike and he thought about Charlie and the good men, like Heller, working on the site, and he thought about the evil that lurked somewhere off in the distance . . . evil that he knew he would have to contend with sooner or later. Then he took one more look off into the horizon at the amazing beauty of "big sky country" and then made his way back down the slope to oversee the final day's operation.

CHAPTER 35

Jake found Mike in the mess tent.

"So what do we have today?"

"A lot better than I had when I was in the service," said Mike, attacking a plate of fried eggs, sausage, and potatoes.

"That looks good. Think I'll get the same thing," and he turned to head toward the mess line when a young woman dressed in Air Force fatigues bearing the insignia of the 341st Mission Support Group stationed at Malmstrom set a tray down and seated herself across from Mike.

At the urging of the President, the Governor of Montana had offered to help with the cleanup, and the 341st had been mobilized and sent to the site. Most of its members had been exchanged for Delta Force. Guarding the perimeter, their military presence tended to effectively keep away sightseers and others who shouldn't be near the site.

Mike looked up and stared at her.

"Can I help you?"

She turned and looked up at Jake and smiled.

"C'mon, Jake," she said, patting the bench beside her. "Have a seat. We need to talk."

Jake slowly took a seat on the bench.

Mike said, "What the hell is going on?" when Joan Phoebe Taylor, the daughter of Benjamin Matthews and the leader of Group 45, turned in his direction and cut him short.

"C'mon, Mike . . . you can't have forgotten Mexico already?"

There was a clatter as Mike's fork hit the tray, and he reached behind him, where his weapon was secured to his belt, keeping his eyes on her the whole time.

"I don't think you want to do that, Mike. Take my word for it. Better yet, take a look at this," and she motioned to a man behind her, dressed in a similar uniform, the face beneath the bill of his cap one of inherent evil. The man came over and held up a small video screen. There was a video playing on the screen.

Mike lunged across the table and put his hands around her throat and hissed, "I'll kill you here and now, you bitch, if you harm a hair on her head, so help me!"

Jake stared at the cell phone and saw the video of Charlotte Kosior, tied to a chair, bound and gagged, and he reached up to Mike's forearms and pulled them until Mike looked at him.

"Sit down, Mike. Sit down."

Hatred and anger pouring over him, Mike stared at Jake and finally let go and collapsed back on the bench while Joan turned her head back and forth and sneered at Mike, "One more move like that, Lang . . . she's dead. Understand me? Dead."

"You heard what I said," replied Mike, now with an eerie, steely calm. "One hair . . . and you die."

"Yeah, I seemed to have heard your threats before. Think you made a couple to my father, too. By the way, what was that young lady's name? Paula . . . Paula something?"

"Don't push it," said Jake. "What do you want?"

"Aw, c'mon boys. I'm just having a little fun. What do I want? I want the treasure. Let's just say certain activities have stifled our cash flow. I think what you boys have found will certainly make up for the loss."

"How'd you even know about this?" asked Mike.

"C'mon, Mike," she said. "You know the answer. We have people everywhere . . . inside . . . on the outside . . . most importantly, I always have people watching you two. We just followed the trail . . . put microphones in the right places . . . bugged phones. We had a pretty good idea what the picture was, and we just let you lead us to it."

CHAPTER 36

"Now, as far as your threats go, Mike, here's the thing . . . I'm sure you would kill me if you could . . . but you can't . . . not as long as I have your little girlfriend. So here's what you two are going to do . . . it's nothing too complicated. I want the three-word passcode for the 8:00 P.M. change tonight. That's all. I'll take care of everything else, and if I get it and it is correct, and my plan works, I will return Ms. Kosior to you with not even a hair disturbed . . . just as you want, Mike. But if they are fake . . . if you contact anyone about this meeting . . . or if anyone in any way tries to stop those trucks from leaving tonight . . . she dies. It's that simple. We understand each other? C'mon boys, a simple 'yes' will do."

Neither Jake nor Mike would speak.

"All right, I get it . . . I get it . . . you're upset. I understand. Now, what's the password?"

Jake stared at Mike and Mike stared back.

"We don't have a choice," said Jake, and he looked back at Joan. "Livingston Saturday Night."

Joan looked at Jake and said, "Jimmy Buffett fan, huh? Well, we are in Montana and it's Saturday. How quaint!"

She stood up.

"I must be on my way, boys. Oh, Jake, one other thing I forgot to mention . . . I will give Mr. Lang back his girlfriend unharmed, but there's a little wrinkle to the delivery. It's in exchange for him delivering you to me."

Mike began to rise up again.

"No way you miserable bitch!"

"It's okay, Mike. It's okay. I'll handle this. Just how will it work?" he asked.

"Simple. A story will be created. Ms. Kosior is needed back here to ensure that everything of value has been packed up and shipped, and you will simply replace her on the helicopter that brings her in . . . and that helicopter will supposedly be taking you to Malmstrom to oversee the operation there, as you did here. Look guys, we could go over and over this, but you know you're going to do what I want. You don't have a choice. Jake's not going to sacrifice Ms. Kosior. If you want Ms. Kosior back, you're not going to stop Jake from doing the right thing. He always does the right thing. I'm really tired of the games you two play. I have to put an end to it. I tried in Mexico. This time I have to make sure. Sorry . . . no hard feelings. That's just the way it is."

"You know I can't let this happen," said Mike.

She looked at him.

"I don't think it's your call," she said. "If all goes well a helicopter will land up on that mesa the same time the last truck is supposed to pull out and Miss Kosior will be on it and she will get out to your waiting arms, Mr. Lang, and you, Jake Sullivan, will get in."

"And, of course," said Jake, "the trucks are going to be driven by your men to destinations unknown."

"As will the military convoys protecting them," she said. "I have thought of everything. Now, I must say goodbye. We all have work to do."

She turned to walk away, then turned back and giggled.

152

"Oh, and one last thing." She again motioned for her hench-man to move forward. "I apologize. I didn't formally introduce my friend. Meet Antonio Ortiz. Antonio, this hothead is Mike Lang, and I think you already know Mr. Sullivan. He's the man who killed your father. Antonio will be accompanying us on our travels, Jake. You two should get to know each other, given your common interests."

Ortiz leaned close to Jake and sneered, "See you soon, Sullivan."

Jake fixed him with a cold stare.

"Just remember, I put Carlos down . . . and I intend to do the same to you."

"Well, enough of the bravado boys . . . we all have things to do."

She again motioned to Ortiz and they walked out of the hut.

CHAPTER 37

Jake and Mike sat at the table, sitting in silence for a long time. Mike was still staring down at his uneaten food on his tray, shaking his head back and forth.

"It's not happening. Not again. I should have been with her!" he said, banging his fist on the table. "I have to save her."

"I know," said Jake, "and we will. This is on me."

"And you can't get on that helicopter."

"I have to, Mike. We have to do everything she wants. It's the only way Charlie will be safe."

"She's going to kill you."

"I know . . . and that's the part I have to figure out . . . that, and how to make sure she doesn't get her hands on what's in those trucks. Listen, Mike, it's obvious she's monitoring all our communications, and how do we . . . out of all this crew . . . how do we know who's working for her and who isn't."

Jake thought about how great the morning had started up on the mesa, looking out over the beauty of the land as far as the eye could see.

"And," he said out loud, *"a large, dark pool of water."*

He looked at Mike.

"I think I have a plan. We need to get to work," and he rose and began heading toward the exit.

Mike followed after him, shaking his head. "Of course you do."

CHAPTER 38

Jake had gone to his quarters and pulled something from his duffle bag. When Mike arrived, he turned it on and easily found the two bugs that had been placed there and then began to explain his plan. When he was done, Mike looked at him.

"Way too risky, Jake. It's a matter of seconds and inches between life and death . . . and that is only if you can get what you need."

"Mike, you said it yourself . . . we can't let another innocent die. We have to save Charlie. There is no other way. Those trucks have to leave and I have to get on that chopper."

Mike looked at him for a long time and then slowly shook his head in the affirmative.

"All right, you win. What do you want me to do?"

Jake looked at his watch.

"In one hour, the operation is supposed to be over. I have to act normal and make sure it's closed down and everything is taken care of, and then I have to get into that cavern . . . alone. You have to make sure it stays that way."

CHAPTER 39

"*It might help,*" thought Jake, as he crawled through the overgrowth at the base of the mesa. Cloud cover had rolled in and the moon was obscured. He made his way on his hands and knees to the edge of the water. He had arranged with Heller to have one of the divers working the last phase of the operation leave his wetsuit on the shore. He found it and quickly changed and donned a mask and waited to slip into the water.

The actual dredging had ended in the morning and the last truck had been loaded and moved into place. By 6:00 P.M., the dredging equipment had been pulled from the river and loaded on flatbeds and was on its way to Malmstrom.

All non-necessary personnel not guarding the perimeter and/ or driving the trucks were pulled out and the engineers were busy taking down the Quonset huts, and by midnight, when the trucks were to pull out, the area would look like they had never been there.

Jake and Mike had stood by helpless when the guard change occurred at 8:00 P.M., as they knew the incoming group were members of Group 45. The truck drivers, the guards . . . everyone, so far as they knew, were the enemy.

Mike was hidden on the opposite shore of the Jefferson and had conducted surveillance of the entire area, and when he was sure that they were alone, he entered a single digit into his phone, the sound of it reaching Jake in his earpiece.

Jake brought down the mask and entered the water as noise-lessly as possible, knowing that, in all probability, there was some-one in the hills around them, watching and listening. All calls were being monitored. It was his hope that they wouldn't be able to monitor the one he was about to make.

CHAPTER 40

The water was frigid, even in his wetsuit, as he slowly slipped under the surface, crawled down the steps, and entered the tunnel. He moved horizontally for approximately thirty yards, when the tunnel ended and a shaft of water rose above him.

There were hand-holds cut into the limestone, and he slowly pulled himself up through the water. Finally, he broke the surface and pulled himself up and onto a limestone ledge.

The caverns were dark. All of the lighting had been removed and his flashlight revealed that everything had been brought back to a natural state, as well as could be done.

The flashlight illuminated the drawings on the walls, the mark of Meriwether Lewis, and he thought about Charlie and how excited she had been, and how she wanted to come here and examine those drawings, and a deep resolve set in and he promised himself that she would do exactly that . . . no matter what the cost. As he panned his flashlight around, everything was gone . . . the gold, the silver, the gems, and the skeletons of the Aztec warriors. All that remained of Montezuma's treasure was the legend. It was as if it had never existed.

He moved away from the opening of the pool, deeper into the cavern, and took an item from a waterproof bag. He held the encrypted phone he had been given during the Branson affair and entered a four-digit number.

"C'mon," he said, "c'mon," as static crackled. Would the cavern provide him cover, or would it make it impossible for the signal to reach its target. It seemed like it took forever, and then, finally . . .

"Is there trouble, Mr. Sullivan?"

"More than you can imagine, Colonel . . . more than you can imagine."

CHAPTER 41

"I'll make this short. My hope is that I've put myself in a position where this call can't be monitored. If it is, all hell is going to break loose."

"Understood," came the reply.

"Here's what's happened, and here's what I need," and he began to explain the day's events.

CHAPTER 42

"Sounds like that lady sure doesn't care for you all that much."

"You could say that. What do you think?"

"I would say you are crazy, except I've done the same thing myself. Let me get to work and see what I can do."

"How will I know?"

"Don't worry, Mr. Sullivan. You'll know."

"Thanks, Colonel. As I'm sure you realize, time is of the essence."

"Always is, isn't it?" and the phone went dead.

On the other end of the line, Colonel Jackson Tillman called out the door, "Sutton! Get in here! We have work to do!"

CHAPTER 43

Mike could see Jake coming out of the water with the night vision goggles he was wearing, and they made their separate ways through the dark as quietly and quickly as possible to the vehicle they would use to leave the camp.

Jake quickly toweled off, changed, and explained what happened to Mike.

"So all we can do is wait?"

"I'm afraid so, but hopefully that wait will be interrupted by Colonel Tillman."

And at approximately 11:00 P.M., it was. Jake and Mike were standing by the bank of the Jefferson, once again tranquil and unspoiled, when a guard making his rounds strolled past. He nodded his head in acknowledgement and then stopped and opened a pack of gum and put a wad in his mouth. Lieutenant Sutton turned and looked at Jake and Mike.

"Sorry, sirs. Might you have the time? Evidently the battery in my watch died. Seems like I've been walking for hours, but it probably hasn't been that long," and shook his head in disgust. "Damn 'Made In China' stuff." As he took it off and went to put it in his pocket, the watch fell silently to the ground.

"It's just after 11:00 P.M. said Mike. Another hour until midnight."

"I thought so," he said. "Oh well. Thank you, sir. Hey, would either of you gentlemen like a piece of gum?"

"No, thanks," said Jake.

"I would," said Mike. "Thanks."

"No problem. I know I'll be chewing this one for a while yet," and he headed off into the night.

Mike opened the gum and seemed to put it in his mouth and then bent down, picked up a stone, and skipped it on the river. With the next stone, he picked up the watch, threw the stone, and put both watch and gum in his pocket and said to Jake, "Let's get out of here and go double check the convoy."

"Yeah, we're about done with our last adventure. Let's go make sure everything is ready to roll."

"I still don't want you getting on that chopper," Mike whispered.

And Jake whispered back, "No choice, my friend. This time she's got us."

What someone watching and listening couldn't see was the smile on Jake's face when he said it.

Around 11:30 P.M., the new team of drivers that had arrived after 8:00, all members of or loyal to Group 45, were again asked for the proper password and were checked and rechecked and assigned their vehicles. The rest of the camp had gone through its final shutdown, was packed up, and ready to depart.

Jake stood before them and thanked them for their service. They didn't know he was especially speaking to one man at the end of the third row, who looked at Jake and gave a small nod, while continuously chewing a wad of gum.

Then they broke formation, entered the waiting troop carriers, and headed out.

CHAPTER 44

Finally, at midnight on the dot, the military convoy took up position at the front and rear of the column of twenty trucks and they pulled out to make their way to Malmstrom.

Their taillights could be seen winding through the hills and over the flatlands for several miles from the top of the ancient temple where Jake and Mike stood, and then, suddenly, the lights all separated and headed off in different directions.

Jake looked at Mike.

"Just about where we figured they'd split up. So far, so good."

"Well, let's hope so . . . if Sutton was able to do what we wanted and mount a GPS locator on every one of them . . . and Delta Force is standing by waiting for our signal."

Just then they heard the sound of rotors, and two pinpoints of light grew brighter as a helicopter approached where they were standing.

CHAPTER 45

Joan Phoebe Taylor, now in flight gear, got out first, followed by Antonio Ortiz, pushing Charlotte Kosior in front of him.

"Let her go!" yelled Mike, over the sounds of the chopper.

"Please, Mr. Lang, we have a deal. All has gone well with the trucks so far, and here stands Mr. Sullivan. Absent any last minute bravado, your little friend will be fine. Ready, Mr. Sullivan?"

Jake turned and looked at Mike, walked over to him, and hugged him . . . and whispered, "Just in case . . . I don't know how . . ." and he stopped.

"I know," said Mike. "Better go."

"What a beautiful sight," said Joan, sarcastically, "now let's go."

Jake turned and headed toward the chopper and Ortiz pushed Charlie toward Mike. She ran the rest of the way and threw herself into his arms.

"Are you all right?" he asked.

She couldn't answer. All she could do was bury her head in his shoulder, and she began to cry.

"What is Jake doing?" she asked, looking up.

"What he always does. He's doing what he has to."

Jake had plastic cuffs put on his hands in front of him and Ortiz pushed him into the rear of the chopper, then got in and sat down beside him. He had been searched and a stick of gum had been found in his pocket.

The rotors of the helicopter turned faster, ready for liftoff from the mesa. The guard was ready to throw the gum away.

"C'mon," Jake said, "last meal, right?" pointing his finger to the gum.

Ortiz looked at it and laughed.

"Yeah, sure. Go ahead, Sullivan. Maybe it will keep you quiet," and he unwrapped the gum and shoved it into Jake's mouth.

With that, Taylor said to the pilot, a large, sullen black man, "Let's go!" and the helicopter rose from the mesa into the night sky.

CHAPTER 46

In his head, Jake began to count, as he had done a hundred times since he initiated the plan, and they began to pass over the Jefferson.

When Ortiz looked out the window, Jake took the gum out of his mouth and stuck it under his seat, as the directions that Sutton had concealed in the packet had told him to do.

"Nice view, isn't it?" Jake said to Ortiz, never losing count in his head.

"Shut up," the guard replied.

"You could use a better class of convict," Jake said to Taylor.

"Oh, don't worry, Mr. Sullivan. You'll find Antonio is as skilled as his father in his work."

"It was you," said Jake. "You're the bastard that tortured Adam Colbert."

"Yeah . . . and I enjoyed the hell out of it . . . but not as much as I will you."

"I don't think so," said Jake. "I think I'll pass," as he hit the number he had been counting toward. "And by the way, say hello to your father in hell."

With that, he kicked out at Ortiz, exacting all his strength, hanging on to a metal rod above his head for leverage and forcing his back against the helicopter wall. Ortiz fell backwards out the open helicopter door, the last sound being his screams as he fell.

Jake slid out the exit feet first and fell into the night, pushing the button on Sutton's watch that he was now wearing, and began to fall.

CHAPTER 47

It all happened in a matter of seconds, but it played over slowly in her brain.

"*The Goddamn gum!*" Joan said to herself, and looked down into space as Jake hit the deep pool of water, almost dead center. "Jake, you son-of-a-bitch," she smiled, just as she and everything around her burst into a huge fireball, illuminating the Montana night.

CHAPTER 48

As soon as Jake hit the water, Sutton, who had donned a wetsuit and remained hidden, was in the pool, cutting off Jake's cuffs and pulling him down into the tunnel, giving him a secondary breathing apparatus. They entered the tunnel as the chopper burst into flames and debris began to rain down into the pool. They stayed there until the wreckage had settled.

Once Sutton got the okay from Mike, he signaled Jake and they surfaced. As they reached the shallows and began to wade out, Jake shivering from the cold, reached out his hand.

"Thank you, Lieutenant, for all your help. What about the trucks."

"Mr. Lang gave the signal, just as you had directed. The GPS lit up like lights on a Christmas tree and Delta was on top of every one of them in a matter of minutes. They got it all, Mr. Sullivan . . . they got it all."

And then he looked up into the night sky.

"Hell of a plan, I must admit . . . hell of a plan."

CHAPTER 49

Mike and Charlie had hidden under an outcropping just below the summit as the chopper departed and stayed there through the explosion and the aftermath, Mike only taking the time to send a signal on the encrypted phone to alert the Delta Force to take action. They had not been able to see Jake jump or land, and all Mike could say when he and Sutton came into view was, "Jake, you crazy son-of-a-bitch! You did it again!"

CHAPTER 50

Lieutenant Sutton got behind the wheel of the Jeep, along with Jake in the passenger's seat, and Mike and Charlie in the back. They were soon speeding along Route 257 heading toward Great Falls and Malmstrom Air Force Base.

Information kept coming in to Sutton as he drove.

"As I told you, all the trucks are accounted for . . . all the perpetrators have been arrested, and a search team is going through the debris of the helicopter."

"I want to know their findings as soon as possible," said Jake.

"She's dead. I watched you fall the whole way, Mr. Sullivan," said Sutton. "No one came after you, but we may have a problem. A man came out before you and grabbed a strut, and then, finally, dropped."

"And?" asked Jake, looking at the side window.

"He might have hit the outer edge of the pond."

"Shit!" exclaimed Jake. "We need confirmation on bodies ASAP!"

"Understood, sir," replied Sutton.

"Jake," said Charlie, trying to diffuse the situation, "I don't know how to thank you. I would have been killed. I just don't know what to say."

"You don't have to say anything, Charlie. Besides, I need someone else to put up with Mike."

"Oh . . . real nice thing to say," said Mike. "You know, we were in danger, too. We were hiding under a rock when that helicopter was falling apart all around us."

"Well, I'm certainly glad you made it out to safety, Mike."

Mike started laughing.

"You should have seen how I shielded Charlie . . . exposing myself to danger."

"I can only imagine," said Jake, looking back at them.

Charlie realized what they were doing.

"Oh, you two . . . please stop. At least you I can make stop," she said to Mike, and gave him a long kiss, and then Mike Lang, for once, became quiet.

MALMSTROM AFB
GREAT FALLS, MONTANA

CHAPTER 51

As soon as they arrived at Malmstrom, they asked to be escorted by Lieutenant Sutton to the lab that had been set up, and they entered what appeared to be a large gymnasium. One end was open and truck after truck were pulling in, dumping their contents over a screened pit where containers were separated from silt and placed on a conveyor belt and sent to various staging areas.

Charlie hugged Jake and gave Mike a peck on the cheek.

"I'll see you later, boys. I have to get to work. I just can't believe this is happening," and she headed off, almost running, in the direction the conveyor belts were moving.

After she had gone, Colonel Jackson Tillman approached them.

"Well, by the looks of you, Mr. Sullivan, I gather your plan was a success?"

Jake looked over to Mike.

"Yeah, thanks to my friend, Mr. Lang, here. Everything worked out just fine."

"I just wanted to let you know Lieutenant Sutton passed on your request to me. We just received word from the search team at the sight . . . it looks like parts of two bodies, badly burned, were recovered. One male and one female is the preliminary word."

"Damn," said Jake, "there should be another body . . . Ortiz." He looked at Mike. "I pushed him out of the chopper . . . he couldn't have made it!"

"I'll get hold of my men and make sure the entire scene is gone over again," said Tillman. "In the meantime, nice work on a successful operation, gentlemen."

"Thanks to you, it was," said Mike, as they both shook hands.

He turned, and as he walked away, they heard him say, "Damn I wish I could have been on that helicopter."

"Well," said Jake, "I better go call Bates and give him the news. Looks like we may be dealing with another Ortiz."

"Don't worry," said Mike, "we took care of the first one. We'll take care of this asshole, too. Now, do what Tillman said and enjoy a great job!"

"Thanks, Mike."

"And by the way, if you don't need me anymore, I think I'm going to go down and find Charlie . . . see how she's doing."

"You do that, Mike. Seriously, I'm happy for you. She seems to be a great girl."

"She is. Thanks for getting her back to me."

"Not a problem, pal . . . not a problem."

As Jake walked through the laboratory, heading toward the communication center, he shook off how tired he was . . . how bruised . . . and smiled that his friend could enjoy happiness with someone he cared about . . . smiled about how lucky he was to be alive and be able to go home to Linda and his girls . . . and smiled that the legacy of Benjamin Matthews had finally come to an end.

EPILOGUE

THE WHITE HOUSE
WASHINGTON, D.C.

CHAPTER 52

It was three weeks later, as Jake and Mike sat with Bates in the Oval Office waiting for President Fletcher to arrive. When he entered the room, they rose to their feet.

"Sit down, gentlemen. Has Jason filled you in?"

"I thought you should do that, sir," said Bates.

"Very well," said the President, taking a seat behind the Resolute Desk. "First, let me thank you two once again for a job well done."

"Thank you, Mr. President," they both replied.

"So far as the treasure . . . it's still being added up. It's worth billions, but we don't know how much. Twenty truckloads of gold, silver, and gems . . ." he said, looking off into the distance. "So far, I tend to agree with Jefferson. I'm not sure that politicians here in Washington have any idea what to do with such amounts, nor would they use it wisely. I can see nothing but political battles, rancor, and waste, given the current political climate in this country. For now, it's been moved to an undisclosed, extremely safe location, where it will continue to be analyzed and cataloged by the person I have named to supervise this project . . . Charlotte Kosior . . . whom I believe you know. It may be a year . . . it may be longer . . . before we sort this all out, and I want to make sure the right thing is done . . . and that a discovery of such historical significance is properly recorded for the ages and used for the good of mankind and not to its detriment.

Now, as for Group 45, we've been hearing rumors that a meeting is being scheduled to select a new leader. We're hoping that those rumors are true. If we discover the time and location, we intend to hit that meeting with everything we have and put an end to Group 45 once and for all. Naturally, I hope you two will be involved, and I will keep you advised of any new information."

"Thank you, Mr. President," said Jake. "We'll be happy to help in any way we can," he said, looking at Mike.

"And I'd also like to thank you, Mr. President, for selecting Miss Kosior to handle the project regarding the treasure. I know how much this means to her."

"You do realize, Mr. Lang, you may not be seeing her for a while?"

"It's her life's work, sir. She'll be happy, and we'll see each other eventually."

"Very well. Is there anything else we need to discuss?"

"If we may, Mr. President," said Jake, looking at Mike again, "we'd like to make a small request as a result of this operation."

The President looked at Bates and smiled.

"At least they're consistent, Jason."

"That they are, Mr. President . . . that they are."

The President sat back in his chair and looked at both of them.

"All right, gentlemen, what do you want this time?"

CHARLOTTESVILLE, VIRGINIA

CHAPTER 53

There was a knock on Nina Colbert's door. An envelope was being delivered to her by a courier of the United States Government.

She opened the door to find a gentleman in a suit and sunglasses standing on her front porch. He took off his sunglasses and smiled at her.

"Mrs. Nina Colbert?"

"Yes. It is."

"Mrs. Colbert, I have something for you . . . a packet of information from the President of the United States."

"The what?" said Mrs. Colbert.

The man smiled again.

"The President, ma'am. He sends you this with his deepest sympathy for the loss of your husband and to inform you that you should be very proud of the service he rendered his country. Here you are."

Her mouth was agape and her eyes were wide open. She couldn't believe what she was hearing, and her hands shook as she took the package from the gentleman, who put on his sunglasses, turned, and walked to the curb, where he got into the passenger's side of a black SUV, windows tinted, that pulled away into the afternoon sun.

She closed the door and made her way to a chair and sat down and opened the packet. There was a letter on White House stationery.

"Dear Mrs. Colbert,

While I am not at liberty to provide you with detailed information concerning your husband's death or the aftermath, I can tell you that I and the rest of the country are extremely proud of his sacrifice.

Accordingly, in recognition of his valor and his contribution, your country would like to provide you with the enclosed.

With deepest respect and sympathy,

Jordan Fletcher
President of the United States"

She looked at the letter a long time, tears welling in her eyes, and she finally set it down and looked at the rest of the packet, which explained that an unlimited account had been set up for her granddaughter, with her as Trustee of that account, to be used for any and all medical testing and/or treatment for the remainder of her granddaughter's life, and there was further notification that she had been accepted into a clinical trial and was being assigned to one of the world's foremost physicians relative to the disease with which she was afflicted.

She put the documents down in her lap and her body began to shake, and the tears increased, and she held her head in her hands and wept, and then very quietly spoke to herself, "You kept your promise, Mr. Sullivan . . . you kept your promise."

MIAMI,
FLORIDA

CHAPTER 54

Jake and Mike had been working steadily for two weeks after they got back. The alert concerning the Port of Miami was still in effect and chatter had increased.

Jess O'Donnell, the Director of Homeland Security, had raised the alert level and was in constant contact with them as the days went on.

Jake was reading through the latest report when Mike entered. He sat down at his desk, put his feet up, locked his hands behind his head, and looked at Jake with a broad grin on his face.

"Would I be correct that you just got a phone call?" asked Jake.

"I did," said Mike.

"How is she?"

"Doing great. Loving the work. Missing yours truly."

"Any idea where she is?"

"Nope. I just know she's safe and happy."

"If I knew that about Linda and the girls, I was always satisfied," said Jake.

"I am, too. I mean, I can't wait to see her . . . but . . . it's just good to know that she's okay."

"Nothing like a happy ending," said Jake.

A few minutes later, he had to rethink those words, as a call from Jess O'Donnell came into the office.

"It's worse than we thought, Jake," said Jess O'Donnell. "It looks like nuclear weapons have entered the country."

NEXT IN THE SERIES...

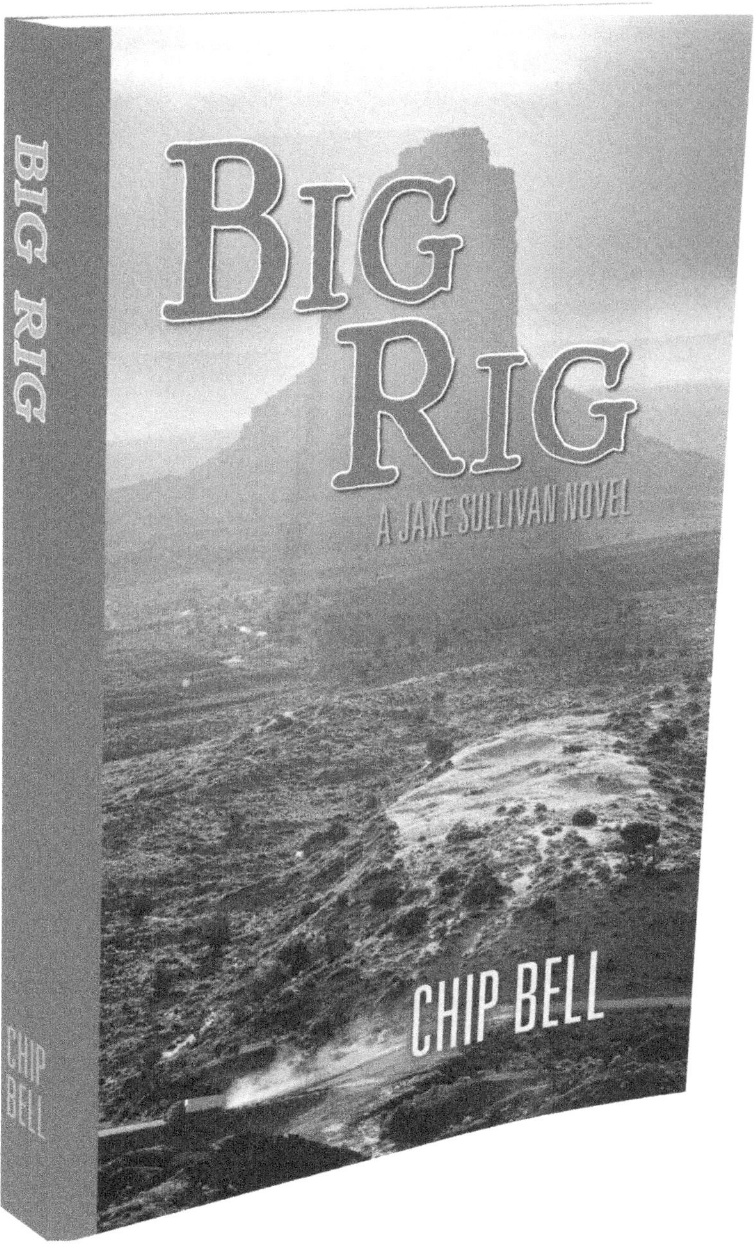
BIG RIG
A JAKE SULLIVAN NOVEL
CHIP BELL
BIG RIG
CHIP BELL

CHIP BELL

1725 FIFTH AVENUE
ARNOLD, PA 15068

724-339-2355

chip.bell.author@gmail.com
clb.bcymlaw@verizon.net
www.ChipBellAuthor.com

 FOLLOW ME ON FACEBOOK
facebook.com/chipbellauthor

 FOLLOW ME ON TWITTER
@ChipBellAuthor

 FOLLOW ME ON PINTEREST
pinterest.com/chipbellauthor
/the-jake-sullivan-series

 **TAKE THE TIME TO REVIEW
THIS BOOK ON AMAZON**
amazon.com/author
/chipbellauthor.com

Made in the USA
Monee, IL
16 May 2025

17595858R00115